Steel Justice

STEEL BOOK SIX

EMPIRES

SERIES

Steel Justice © 2021
by J.L. Gribble

Published by Dog Star Books
Bowie, MD

First Edition

Cover Image: Bradley Sharp
Book Design: Jennifer Barnes

Printed in the United States of America

ISBN: 978-1-947879-34-8

Library of Congress Control Number: 2021936103

www.RawDogScreaming.com

Also from the Steel Empires Series

Steel Justice

J.L. Gribble

Toria Connor assumed the Mercenary Guild's official guidelines frowned upon the client protecting the bodyguard. But when the body was a genuine weredragon, over ten feet long from snout to tail, with talons the length of daggers, the official guidelines could sod off. "Zhinu, watch your left!"

The blue dragon lunged to the side, catching another robotic dog with her claws and crushing its bladed fist. The knives crumpled in her grip like tin foil. That took care of one attack method, but it caught Zhinu's forelimb with its frontal limbs. Metal pounded her scales, and Zhinu hissed through her fangs at the brute force of the blows.

"We have to get out of here, Tor!" Kane swept his blade at another robot, throwing his weight behind the blow. Sparks flared, and the robot jerked to the side. It crashed against the window glass, where spiderweb cracks formed.

Toria dropped to one knee as the fifth limb swiped in her direction, and she used both hands to force her sword point into another exposed joint. This time, she threaded power through the blade itself. The energy met no resistance, and the machine froze mid-movement as Toria's magic fried the electronics with prejudice. She wrenched her sword away as the construct collapsed, unable to compensate for its unbalanced state.

The harsh tang of burnt plastic mixed with ozone swept through the room. Toria sneezed.

Her brief moment of inattention almost proved fatal. One of the robotic dog forms waiting in reserve crept forward at its brethren's demise. This one did not have a fifth limb extending from its torso and instead used one of its legs to sweep at Toria's crouched form. Zhinu launched herself at the creature. They skidded across the floor in a tangle of limbs, biological and mechanical, until they collided with the table holding the computer.

The screen toppled and shattered, but the beeping continued unceasingly.

The countdown ticked lower.

One month ago

Toria rolled over in bed, stretching her bare skin against the sateen sheets. Even more luxurious, a deft hand drifted across her back. Liam's fingers teased her with a caress, but she purred when he dug them into the persistent muscle knots at the base of her spine.

Liam's breath tickled her shoulders. "You keep those sounds up, and we'll never get out of here on time."

"We shouldn't even be in bed," Toria said. She squinted against the late afternoon sunlight creeping across her room.

Their room. Liam had brought the bedsheets from his apartment, and a second dresser now squeezed alongside hers in the loft bedroom. They had decided to cohabitate spur of the moment to coincide with the end of Liam's lease in downtown Limani. Why should he pay rent when Toria's rooms at the mage school would soon stand empty? Hopefully he felt free to do some consolidation and reorganization in her absence.

Liam's fingers continued to knead at Toria's muscles. "How are you still this tense, after…." He let the unspoken words trail off as if embarrassed to put a name to their recent activities, but the amusement that danced in his face was far from coy.

"Trust me. I'm relaxed." With great reluctance, Toria pulled away from Liam's warm touch. "Just… anxious."

Toria hated to break the routine they had fallen into the past months. But work called, and her days of coming home to shower and tempt Liam away from his research for an afternoon rendezvous would soon end. Nothing lasted forever, especially not perfection.

She paused at the edge of the bed. The sun kissed Liam's torso, golden against the ivory sheets. Eight months ago, she had despaired of ever seeing him again. But she traveled through the shadows of time to find him waiting, and she would never take a single moment with him for granted.

Liam smoothed the wrinkled skin between her eyes with a fingertip. "You're making me feel like I should be relaxing you again, but I'm not sure I have the strength."

Laughing, Toria pressed a kiss to his palm. "I'm sure you'd find it somewhere. But the guys are waiting for us for dinner."

Their standing weekly double-date with the other half of Toria's warrior-mage pair and his partner was sacrosanct. She checked the clock above the curtained entryway that separated her sleeping area from the loft's larger living space. Archer finished his class with the current crop of apprentices soon. Kane should have showered in peace after their sparring practice at the Mercenary Guildhall.

Well, Toria had spent the first half of her shower in peace. She tugged a hand through her mass of half-dried locks and envied Liam's close-cropped blond hair. "You get dressed. I'm going to dunk my head again."

With one last appreciative scan across Liam's body, ending with his knowing smirk, she darted into the bathroom to rerun her shower. She stepped under the hot water for a quick rinse, and Liam's voice carried across the tile. "Do you want the silver top that came yesterday?"

"No, thank you," she called, turning off the water. As she twisted her shoulder-length hair to wring out excess water, she said, "I ordered that specifically for Londinium. Though I'm sure Zhinu will force me into shopping for the latest styles with her as soon as we step off the ship."

Anxiety jolted through Toria again at the sudden reminder of how things would soon change. She once thought returning home from Nacostina would restore her equilibrium, but on occasion, this fierce, unpredictable fear was her new normal. She wrapped a towel around herself and stepped out of the bathroom, shaking away the jitters under her skin as much as possible.

Liam buttoned a shirt that brought out the blue in his eyes. "I don't know why Archer insisted on this restaurant. You wouldn't think anything with a dress code would appeal to him."

"The owners have a child who has exhibited magical ability, but they're talking about sending him to Fort Carolina for training in a few years," Toria said. "Archer is on a mission to prove his respectability." Even if it meant dragging his family to a formal restaurant when their usual meals out involved someplace with less class and more beer options.

She collected clean undergarments from her dresser and dropped the towel to the floor once inside the walk-in closet. The silver blouse hung next to the rest of the new clothing purchased in preparation for the job in Londinium. Lady Zhinu Wallace was officially coming out for her first Season as the wife of Earl Robert Wallace. Though the lady in question had no practical need for bodyguards, her status as a nobleman's wife demanded it. Therefore, Zhinu had requested Toria and Kane's services, preferring personal friends who would treat her with respect and ensure that she did not face the brunt of the British nobility without allies at her side. Toria foresaw less comfortable times ahead, both physically and mentally, so she wrapped herself in comfort now in the form of a tunic over knit leggings.

She shut the closet door on the new purchases, reminding herself for the third time that week to haul her trunk out of storage. Once, she chose what to bring on long contracts as an adventure in playing "what if." Now, it seemed more a chore to put off for later. But their departure date neared, and she was running out of later.

Signs of spring abounded outside in the form of buds on trees, but Kane had not spent the extra time needed to prepare the gardens for his departure. As if the comforts of home or lure of family had also muffled his urge for the next great adventure. Or did she project her anxiety on her partner rather than confront her own?

"Hey." Liam placed a finger under Toria's chin and tilted her face to his. "You okay?"

Even after months, the casualness of modern-day Liam sometimes jarred with her memories of Liamacorin, stuffy museum curator. "I'm fine." She pulled away.

The elven man stayed close on her heels as they left the bedroom. He kept silent while they pulled on shoes but stopped Toria with a gentle hand on her arm when she gripped the knob to the loft's exterior door. "You're not fine."

Her fingers tightened, but she forced an otherwise relaxed pose. They were a couple on their way out for an enjoyable evening with their two best friends. What could be wrong?

But it wasn't in her to lie to Liam, so she dropped her hand and sagged against the door. "I'm not fine. I'm excited to get back to work, to a long-term job. To see Zhinu and Rob and help Zhinu through this time in her life. But this isn't going to be like the trips Kane and I took south over the winter. I'll be gone for months, and I'll miss you." A thin slice of her emotional layer cake, but one easiest to serve.

The words hung in the air between them, and Toria braced for Liam's response. He had spent decades without her, and she dared complain of a six-month-long separation?

Liam bit his bottom lip, thinking.

Toria's skin flushed under the intensity of Liam's gaze, and she averted her face as if he had the power of a vampire.

"I'll miss you, too," Liam said, finally. "But this is different than when I waited before."

"How so? I'm leaving you again."

"But this time, you'll know me." Liam tugged Toria away from the door and into his embrace. "This time, I won't spend years waiting for you to be born. For you to grow up. For you to remember me. This time I know, without a shadow of a doubt, that I will be in your thoughts. That I am known to you, and that I'm not the only one looking forward to us being together again."

Toria buried her face in Liam's neck, relishing the mingled scent of spiced tea, of him, of them. He had always been honest with her in past conversations, and she heard clearly what he did not remind her of now. That he'd had other lovers in the years between. That more than once, he'd sworn to stay far away from Limani and any chance they would meet again. But in the end, he'd manipulated the events that forced their first meeting. And then he had stayed, memory and his natural curiosity forcing him to give what they found in the past a real chance in the present. "It can't be that easy."

"It's not easy. But it's easier with you." Liam pressed a kiss to Toria's forehead. "We do need to go to dinner now. Or Archer and Kane will come fetch us and express their disappointment that they cannot mock us for being caught abed."

"That's not how it works," Toria said as she pulled out of Liam's arms. They left the loft over the former stables and clattered down the external wooden staircase. "You know I live out here instead of in the main house because I got tired of always knowing when those two were going at it." Some elements of the magical bond between Kane and Toria extended miles. Luckily, the echoes of certain physical sensations had a much shorter distance threshold.

"Then I shall have to ply you with wine at dinner, so they have reason to mock us afterward." Liam laced his fingers with hers as they followed the path that wound around the mage school, where they would meet Kane and Archer at the front door.

"Like you need to ply me with anything to get into bed with you," Toria said. "But unfortunately, I have that meeting with Mom later tonight."

"Right. You have the radio?"

"It's already packed."

After dinner, Toria deposited the guys at the mage school, where the three had plans to find out how far they could get in a new co-op video game before the application of alcohol made playing more of a chore than a challenge. Most evenings included Toria in this plan, but the guys had designated her the responsible adult tonight. Because after dinner, she had a second date—one even more nerve-wracking than keeping Kane, Archer, and Liam on their best behavior for a prospective student's parents.

She hauled the heavy backpack out of the battered vehicle and slung it over her shoulder, then slammed the trunk closed and ascended the porch steps of the manor house where she grew up. The mage school might be where she lived now, but she let herself in the front door without knocking because her parents had made it clear that this would always be home.

The house's vampiric residents knew of her arrival as soon as she turned the town-car into the driveway, but she called out a hello to her father as she passed through the main floor of the house.

Jarimis stirred a cup of tea in the entryway to the kitchen, posh in slacks paired with a knit sweater. "Mikelos is out for the evening."

That explained the lack of shouted return greeting. "You look dressed to go out, too," Toria said. The vampire she had grown up on stories of, and then grown to be friends with since his return to Limani, followed her into the library.

"Your mother and I have an appointment with the current chair of the university's history department, and I wish to put my best foot forward." He settled on the couch in the seating area of the library, careful not to jostle his tea.

Toria placed the backpack on a nearby low table and dropped into an armchair facing it. Jarimis continued to refuse to utter the new name of the university that he had founded, hating that the city renamed it in his honor. For a while, he'd even insisted that he had no interest in returning to teach there. It seemed things had changed over the past eight months. "Good luck with that."

Her adopted mother, the vampire Victory, strolled into the library and sat next to Jarimis. She had not dressed for a job interview, but then again, Victory never dressed for anyone except herself. "How was dinner?"

"Food was good, atmosphere was stuffy," Toria said. "One of the owners did deign to stop by the table and ask how we were enjoying ourselves, so Archer was delighted."

But Toria had not visited tonight to give a restaurant review, and Victory knew it. Her mother leaned forward to nudge at the backpack. "New project?"

"Something like that. I'd rather wait for Grandpa." Better to explain all at once after each vampire arrived than risk repeated questions. Toria unzipped the backpack and withdrew the metal case. She had buffed out most of the rust and scratches that marked the radio's age but had not risked total deconstruction of the device to hammer out the dent on one side.

Asaron drifted in right at that moment. "Haven't seen one of those in a long while."

True to his curious nature, Jarimis leaned forward to inspect the instrument while Asaron sat next to him. "I recognize it… from after the Last War?" Jarimis asked.

"Thereabouts," Toria said. "I dug it out of storage at the mage school." Right out from under her loft, in fact. During their time in Limani, Kane often assisted Archer with the mage apprentices. Toria preferred to work with kids who had air talent, the elemental alignment closest to her own storm, which occurred few and far between in those with magical ability. When not training with Kane or others at Limani's Mercenary Guildhall, she found productive occupation elsewhere that stemmed from her collegiate technical training.

Like tinkering with antiques, such as this radio. "I found this last year, and I poke at it every once in a while, in between other projects. Mostly it decorates the mantel in my living room. Archer said he'd build me a forge on the property in exchange for teaching the fire apprentices, but I'm not ready for that level of commitment yet." Maybe when Mohinder and Sydney hit their teenage years, and she could strangle the angst out of them free from the guilt of making children cry. "Thank you for meeting me here this evening. I know my call yesterday was a bit disjointed."

"You woke me from a sound sleep just past noon," Victory said. "I did not understand your babbled message, but here we are, as you requested."

Toria had wanted to meet with them all at once, but she first shared her news with Liam, and then Kane and Archer, before approaching the vampires. She flipped a metal switch on the radio, and it emitted static and white noise.

Normal sounds for such equipment missing the intricate adaptive device mounted on top—basis for the elven enchantment that would allow it to function. Toria checked the grandfather clock in the corner. Showtime.

The static faded away, replaced by a low hiss. "A moment or so more," Toria said. As if on cue, music blared from the speaker. She jerked forward to adjust the volume to a more manageable level. The theme music faded, replaced by a young man's voice.

"Good evening, and welcome to another installment of Radio Free 101. I'm your host, Matt Elliot, and tonight we're kicking off with a tune requested by my roommate.

He said he'd do the dishes if I played this, so the sink better be clear when I get home, Remi!" After a few seconds of dead air, the opening strains of a Parisiian pop song emerged, and Toria lowered the volume again.

The three vampires stared at the radio as if it might bite them. Victory spoke first. "You fit the device that holds the elven charm inside the radio? And now you can hear the amateur broadcast from the university farther north in Lenapenn. I'm not sure what the big news is."

"There's no elven charm on this radio. And that's not all." Toria had also assumed the show came from Lenapenn when she first got the radio working. After she heard the name of the student's location, she scared the daylight out of him in the middle of a show after hunting him down on campus. His salvaged equipment also had none of the elven magical enhancements needed for most technology to function. "There's no magic at all. And Matt doesn't live in Lenapenn. He goes to school at Jarimis University." And the university did not have the tech necessary for a radio station separate from the one in downtown Limani.

Jarimis flinched at the name even as Victory and Asaron froze where they sat, the full implication of her statement sinking in.

"But—" Asaron cut off his protestation with a scoff.

"Yeah. I tested another old radio in storage at the Mercenary Guildhall. And the one always breaking at the customs house. Both worked." Toria had called her mother in a panic before sharing her information with the guys, who'd reassured her she wasn't going crazy. Archer had checked, and double-checked, the lack of magic.

A song sung by a teenage Parisiian star should not sound ominous, but the bright chords jangled in Toria's ears. She patted the radio. "I think any last remnants of the fading elven world spell are gone. Tech is back."

Vampires did not need to breathe, but Toria caught the hissing exhale as Asaron forced his entire body to relax. He switched the radio off, plunging the library into silence. But Toria ached to talk about this with people who had lived in the world for centuries before the elves cast the spell that limited humanity's ability to execute extraordinary violence upon itself. The reasoning behind the world spell had been an abstract concept for so long—until she found herself trapped in Nacostina with no way home two days before a hydrogen weapon wiped the city off the map. Now, the ruins of the once-vibrant city she had come to love in a few short months sat abandoned in the Wasteland to the west of Limani.

"I won't ask whether you're sure," Victory said. She raised a hand before Toria could make a token defense of her knowledge. "And it's obvious from this broadcast that the word is out if even college students are using tech without elven assistance."

"If the young ones are taking advantage, who knows what progress the political powers have already made," Asaron said. He interlaced his fingers and leaned forward, studying the radio as if it might explode in his face at any moment.

"Technological advances always start with the military, after all," Jarimis said.

For much of its history, the city of Limani had maintained a precarious existence. But it had blossomed when accorded real political power as the neutral zone between British and Roman colonial lands on the New Continent coast, since the Wasteland to the west prevented further expansion. The Romans had jostled that balance a few years ago when the new emperor attempted to invade the city as an expression of power. Limani held firm to its independence, though not without sacrifice. But unlike the major world powers—Roman, British, Qin, and the smaller empires in the southern hemisphere—Limani had no standing military. Limani did not even have a dedicated diplomatic corps. Limani had a city council that settled zoning disputes and coordinated certain imports and exports.

Even the famed university was more well known for its philosophy and history departments than the physical sciences. When Toria considered retiring from her merc career, she envisioned herself in a lab there, reinvigorating the chemistry and physics departments.

The mental image of herself in a lab coat seemed younger every time she imagined it.

"I need to send some messages," Victory said. She crossed to Jarimis' desk in the corner of the library and rustled through the papers. "Jarimis, did you hear from Kahina already, or should I telegraph again?"

Asaron rose from his seat and exited the room without a word.

Instead of answering Victory, scribbling away at his desk, Jarimis raised an eyebrow at Toria. "Leaving for Londinium soon, aren't you?"

"Yep."

"Make sure you get all your notes to me beforehand. I want to review your observations."

Toria raised her own eyebrow in a direct mockery of Jarimis' attention on her. "Do you imply my methodology is flawed?"

"I can't know that until I review your notes, can I?" Jarimis asked. "Or has the peer review process passed out of favor since my day?"

"Nah, still a thing," Toria said. "Think I'm just jealous that I have to stand around and be decorative overseas while you have all the fun."

"You're welcome to stay here and work with me."

His statement drew Victory's attention. "No, she can't. She and Kane are under contract."

Toria pointed to her mother. "That. What Mom said."

Jarimis twisted a pen between his fingers. "One day, you will no longer be able to resist the lure of academia."

"After working so hard for such cushy mercenary gigs?" Toria forced levity into her voice as she gathered the bag in which she'd transported the radio. "Bite your tongue."

All-encompassing relief suffused Kane, tension draining from his muscles when he stepped off the *Lady Sidereus* at Londinium's port. Solid earth under his feet once more, a sensation he would never take for granted however many times he crossed the ocean. He broke away from the crowds streaming toward the luggage retrieval area to a clear expanse of wall, Toria by his side. She gave him the time he needed to release the more durable shields he maintained while shipboard and once again connect with the ground. Her excitement to see their friends vibrated through their magical link.

He needed no words to alert Toria when he completed the quiet ritual. She could sense his rooted emerald shields as intimately as he felt the delicate violet prisms that spun around her. She tossed a half-grin over her shoulder, and he grasped the hand she extended to follow her amidst the crowds.

Thanks to their long-standing friendship with the shipping franchise heir, Kane and Toria did not have to join the throngs searching for their luggage. Instead, the pair ducked into a side corridor to a quieter lounge. There, they could wait for their trunks in peace, sip the first of many cups of tea they would consume on this job, and await retrieval by the driver who would bring them to the large townhouse the Wallace family kept in Londinium.

As they entered the lounge, a broad-shouldered man and the petite woman by his side turned from the window to greet them. Earl Robert Wallace awaited them along with his wife Lady Zhinu, for whom the earl had contracted Kane and Toria to protect during the next six months.

Toria let out a barely contained squeal. She dropped the pack from her shoulder and rushed across the lounge. Zhinu met her in the center of the room. The two women embraced, already exchanging exclamations of how much they had missed each other since the last time the warrior-mage pair had passed through the city over a year ago.

Kane reinforced his shields once more against the surrounding urban center's magical miasma and stepped forward to grasp the earl's extended hand.

Rob's expression lit with pleasure. "Wonderful to see you again, Kane. It's such a reassurance to know that Zhinu will have friends at her side."

"It's our pleasure, sir." And it was a genuine pleasure, even disregarding the handsome amount of money Rob insisted accompany their contract. "We were not expecting to meet you until we arrived at your townhouse."

"Oh, that's my fault." Zhinu withdrew from Toria and hugged Kane in turn before tucking herself once more under Rob's arm. "I insisted we greet you here because I already scandalize the staff at Rob's house enough. Didn't want to think of them tutting behind me when I hugged you both if we'd met at the house."

Genuine happiness radiated from Rob as he clutched his wife. "And it was my pleasure to indulge my bride."

The last time Kane had worked in Londinium, he provided security to a newly monied businessman as decent-paying work. At the same time, Toria had acted as Zhinu's companion during a tour of the northern mountains with other female members of Rob's family—the men, by tradition, discouraged from attending the excursion. At the time, Zhinu still had one semester of graduate school left, though the couple had married after her graduation, as promised in their prenuptial contract.

"Congratulations again," Kane said to Zhinu, referring to both the marriage and the newly conferred degree.

Zhinu dipped her chin in appreciation. "Thank you."

After a perfunctory knock, the lounge door opened behind Kane. Already in the mental space for protection duty, he spun on his heel and prepared to draw his sword. Next to him, Toria extended her bare hand, and energy-adrenaline-intensity surged through their mental link.

The porter who entered, tugging the cart loaded with the pair's luggage, did not appear to note the immediate threat to his life. Rob clapped Kane on the shoulder, a silent signal to stand down, and he approached the porter, already providing directions to where the town-car waited to ferry the group to the couple's city residence.

Toria lowered her hand. "Well, aren't we jumpy?" Her summoned energy dissipated through Kane's connection with the earth, tingling through his toes.

"And you're not on the clock yet, friends." Rob hoisted Toria's traveling pack onto his shoulder and extended an elbow to its owner. "Let's enjoy at least one meal together this evening before we put you to work."

Kane froze for half a beat. Rob—nobleman, businessman, alpha werewolf—should not be carrying anyone's bags, much less one belonging to an employee. But he relaxed when Toria placed her palm into the crook of Rob's arm. He scooped up his bag at the room's entrance and copied Rob's chivalrous action. Zhinu allowed him to escort her out.

Into the swirling mass of bodies still crowding the port building. Rob and Toria, with their paler features, blended into the landscape at once, another pair of travelers. Zhinu and Kane, however, drew immediate stares as passersby halted around them to whisper behind upraised hands. They cut a striking figure—the tall man with skin too brown to be a simple tan escorting the woman with midnight-black hair. Here, it was everything that made her Qin that forced Zhinu to stand out in the crowd, not the striking sapphire eyes that marked her as a weredragon. A handful of other black-skinned folks dotted the crowd, but Zhinu, hailing from a people who once waged war against the British to the point of worldwide destruction, remained an anomaly.

A few braver people nearby dared to wave to Zhinu, who accepted their greetings with a graceful smile and a raised hand of her own. She spoke to Kane like the old friend he was, delight plastered on her face as if they discussed the weather. But Kane noted the strained tone beneath her light words. "It was the wedding of the season, of course. Everyone wanted to see Rob with his foreign bride. In Oxenafor, I was an exciting new student. But here in Londinium, I'm tabloid-fodder. People are waiting for the Qin princess who fled her empire to betray her new people in the same way."

"Have there been more letters?"

"Not that I'm aware. I think the family is protecting me even more after the wedding, now that I'm a legitimate member of the Wallace clan instead of the secret fiancée of the man hosting my attendance at school."

Zhinu had written to her friends often during her first semester of classes, sharing her distress at the hate mail received during her early months in the foreign land. Kane and Toria had ridden out their time as mercenary journeymen by acting as Zhinu's bodyguards whenever the Wallace family, who had embraced Zhinu as one of their own without hesitation, felt she needed the additional protection. Zhinu's ability to transform into a weredragon, unlike any other female of her kind, was a guarded secret, and no one wanted the drama that reveal might bring. Despite the protected status of all weredragons in Qin, the emperor had been willing to let a girl from an illegitimate line flee when he had a brewing civil war to keep his attention. That perspective might change if Zhinu's abilities became common knowledge.

Kane and Toria had spent years, off and on, researching what they could about Zhinu's unique power. But they could only do so much without making it evident why they sought the information.

His mind sped through plans upon contingency plans as they followed Rob and Toria. Zhinu as Lady Zhinu Wallace was not the first high-profile bodyguard contract of their career. Not even the first bodyguard contract for a genuine friend. But Zhinu's position in British nobility made her a unique case. Now, half his job would be to help her wrangle social events during the parliamentary session, not keep Toria from doing too much of Zhinu's science homework.

A sleek silver vehicle waited for the quartet outside of the port entrance. The driver stood by to open the door, but he allowed Rob and Kane to help the ladies inside. Kane resisted the urge to check for all their luggage, even when Toria's attention flicked to the rear of the electric town-car as well. Rob's staff, and Rob's money, ensured no mistakes.

Rob and Zhinu cuddled together on one bench seat, trading comments about what the house chef might prepare for dinner. Toria interrupted with, "That's not necessary—"

"Nonsense." Zhinu waved her off. "Let us treat you as guests for your first night here." The steel in her gaze brooked no argument.

These were friends. Not new clients who didn't understand how mercenaries worked, how the bodyguard relationship worked, how the warrior-mage link worked. Kane's shoulders eased.

He followed along with the flow. They arrived at the townhouse Rob and Zhinu shared "in Town," and settled into the private suite he would share with Toria. As invited, they enjoyed the exceptional dinner provided by the house chef. After dinner and a dessert that would have Kane doubling his cardio the next morning, the two pairs retired to the lounge.

Rob gestured with his glass of scotch to a low table between the couches, covered in arranged papers. "As much as I'm enjoying this evening, we should discuss formalities before your contract starts tomorrow morning. Did either of you have questions or concerns regarding the documents I sent you?"

As one, Kane and Toria responded in the negative. Toria leaned over the table to examine the paperwork, but Kane stood too tall to read that way in comfort. He dropped onto a couch, careful not to jostle his brandy.

The papers consisted of a copy of their mercenary contract, a schedule of events for the next few weeks, and two lists of names. The top of one list read *Friend*, but the second read *Foe*. Kane lifted the second list to read it in detail. Surnames followed by ranks, positions, and personal information, listed in no apparent order Kane could discern. He passed the list to Toria and asked, "I hope you do not intend foe literally."

Zhinu and Rob had settled on the opposite couch, and she elbowed her husband. "I told you it was overdramatic."

"It's a mix of people I'd like you two to be on the watch for," Rob said, ignoring his wife. "Some are people I know personally, who have made no secret of their dislike for my marriage. Others are known senders of some of Zhinu's hate mail, though much has passed through more anonymous channels, which makes it harder to identify. You might encounter some of them during the events Zhinu already has planned in the next few weeks."

Toria asked, "And the friends?"

"People vetted by Wallace security," Rob said.

"What Rob means is people you can be more relaxed around. For example, if I'm sharing tea with Lady Yakira and her daughters or Sir Adair," Zhinu pointed out the names, "you don't have to be quite as on edge as you might be otherwise."

Kane did recognize at least one name on the list of friendlies, which spurred a question. "Does anyone other than Lord Reynolds know about your ability, Zhinu?"

"My parents and sister," Rob said. "No one else in the Wallace family."

"One trusted friend from university," Zhinu said. "You remember meeting Teagan, Toria? Or I suppose it's Lady Teagan, these days, since she married."

"Right, the werewolf you used to run with in the countryside," Toria explained for Kane's benefit. "Teagan's a spitfire. Hell, I'd trust her with my life, too. But do you believe the secret is safe? Lord Reynolds is a nice enough guy, but do you think he didn't tell his superiors in the diplomatic corps at once? That the *queen* doesn't know the Qin weredragon princess on her island isn't what she seems?"

The couple exchanged a wary expression at Toria's questions, then Rob answered her. "We have reached an agreement with Lord Reynolds in exchange for his silence."

When that did not seem to be the answer Toria wanted, Zhinu elaborated. "We bribed him."

"A bought man can be bought a second time," Kane said.

"Which is why we haven't bribed him with money or other tangible goods." Rob chewed on his lower lip, an unexpected sign of insecurity from the suave werewolf. "Ben is a lifelong bachelor, but his niece is estranged from her parents. We helped establish a trust fund for her that his siblings cannot touch, along with a current account she can access for assistance with school fees. Val thinks it's a scholarship for her writing."

Kane raised both palms in resignation. "I will have faith in the arrangement you've created and speak of it no more."

At that, the conversation turned to a review of Zhinu's engagements over the next week. At least four teas, two of which she would host at the Wallace house. Suppers at clubs and private residences. One formal ball to kick off the political season. Their social and political status demanded the couple make appearances at other galas and fetes almost every evening.

Stranger appointments peppered the social obligations of the fresh-minted Lady Zhinu Wallace. Zhinu had committed herself to be more than a decorative wife who existed to bear heirs for her husband—a genetic impossibility between them. The list consisted of visits to Wallace businesses and lands throughout Londinium and the surrounding areas, such as tours of technological laboratories, art galleries, and historical societies. Such disparate holdings were a credit to the Wallace economic strength, and many of the names next to the businesses indicated a family relation. But not all, such as Dr. Meredith Tierney of Foundry Laboratories and Baronet Lemuel Dias of Peters and Sons Shipping and Imports.

Kane collected the schedule and various lists. "May we take these?"

"These copies are for you," Rob said. "If you need any other information, Zhinu knows how to get in contact with my secretary."

"And I'm pretty sure Niko can find out anything up to and including Her Majesty's favorite pair of slippers," Zhinu said. She finished the last of her port and left the empty glass on a side table.

Kane set his empty brandy snifter next to hers, even as habit urged him to bring it to the kitchen so he could wash the glasses himself. But in a proper gentleman's home, such jobs did not fall to the lady of the house's security detail. Tomorrow morning, the mental gear shift would kick in.

They exchanged good evenings with Rob and Zhinu, and Kane followed Toria upstairs. "You good?" his partner asked him. "Job starts tomorrow."

"I'm good," Kane said. "We're lucky we get to work with friends."

Toria set the papers on the desk in their suite's shared parlor. She would stay up late to review them because Kane would fall asleep at once. He needed to regain the energy spent maintaining extensive shielding on the ocean crossing.

Kane pressed a kiss to Toria's hair and departed for his bedroom. He drifted asleep to the familiar noises of Toria rustling papers and scratching notes amidst the rumble of the surrounding city.

Toria's mother loved to tell of her first dinner with Zhinu in her cousin's court in the Qin colonial city Jiang Yi Yue. How Zhinu had insisted that Victory change her outfit to be more appropriate, despite how the tall, pale vampire would never blend into the background regardless of what she wore.

Time and circumstance had changed the young woman.

Zhinu and Rob descended the townhouse stairs, each the perfect image of modern British fashion. Zhinu zeroed in on Toria first. "Oh, that blouse is stunning on you. I'm so glad I guessed the size right."

"You did, for both of us," Toria said.

Of course, some things would not change. Zhinu had stocked Toria and Kane's closets with clothing for the formal events they would be attending. The evening before, she had pointed out that their financial compensation for this contract was for their time and protection, not meant to force them to outfit themselves according to her schedule. Thus, despite the extensive shopping before leaving Limani, Toria donned the sapphire blouse of raw silk that matched Kane's waistcoat. Together, they made a striking pair who complemented Zhinu's gown, a distinct matched set that highlighted the blue of Zhinu's eyes and nails, evidence of her weredragon blood. Rob's tuxedo might have been drab in comparison, but he broke the sharp lines with a pocket square of the same blue hue.

That morning, Toria had caught up one-on-one with Zhinu while Kane ran a few miles around the neighborhood—scoping out the lay of the land, which he reported to his partner in detail over a private lunch while Zhinu ate with her secretary. In the afternoon, Kane supervised while Toria and Zhinu sparred, both of them evaluating the state of their charge's hand-to-hand combat skills. Their primary function as bodyguards was to remove the body from harm's way as soon as possible. However, it never hurt to make sure the body could protect herself if necessary, in instances where Zhinu could not shift to dragon from.

And tonight, the real work began.

The real work also bored the hell out of Toria more often than not.

She stood at Kane's side while they did their best to hold up a portion of the ballroom wall. Her partner's attention remained on Rob and Zhinu as the couple danced across the center of the room, in a pair and with other partners as politeness and political strategy dictated. Toria people-watched because she had less shame when it came to staring down those who gaped at her taller partner.

"I think that wallflower is working up the courage to proposition you."

Kane's attention on Zhinu did not waver, but he asked, "The one in the pink gown?"

"Yes. She keeps looking at you, and now her blush is the same color as her dress."

"Probably because she knows you're watching her."

"I don't think she even notices me next to your attractiveness." Toria kept the smirk off her face, though her sarcasm, meant for Kane's ears alone, dripped loud and clear. Neither of them stood out in the multicultural hodgepodge that populated much of Roman territory. However, Kane attracted more attention in Britannia, especially in the werewolf nobility's upper echelons, who traced their lineage to people from more northern climates.

At least no one at this ball had asked Kane to fetch them a new drink. There was a reason the partners dressed to emphasize their client, not attempt to fade into the background. A lesson learned early in their careers.

The woman in pink vanished between one scan of the room and the next, and Toria hoped she found another person to occupy her interest. She cocked an eyebrow and shook her head at a trio of young noblemen. She preferred to warn them off from a distance instead of declining a dance or a drink with the unlucky fellow who wandered over.

Word would spread soon enough of Zhinu's bodyguards, since some of the nobility in the room did recognize the warrior-mages and extended respectful regards from a distance. A former client even dispatched a footman to deliver coffee to the pair since they would not partake of the champagne that circled the room.

Toria savored her coffee's chocolatey flavor. "Someone loves me and wants me to be happy."

"I bet it was Lord Napier," Kane said. "He knows about your mocha habit."

"But Sir Fulton is the one who first kept us supplied with coffee during late-night rounds, and I spotted him dancing earlier."

They continued a quiet conversation about former clients and their potential current whereabouts for the next few rounds of dancing until Zhinu crossed the floor to them. Kane stepped to the side, and Zhinu leaned between them. Toria plucked a glass of champagne off the tray of a passing footman and passed it over.

"Bless you." Zhinu also accepted Kane's handkerchief and dabbed it at her temples to dry the sweat that shimmered on her skin. "I haven't danced this much in ages. Focusing on all the proper steps is difficult enough when I'm not wearing heels."

Kane took his handkerchief back and shoved it in a pocket. "You've looked lovely, though."

"Why, thank you, kind sir." Zhinu sipped her drink. "Think anyone will care if I ditch the shoes?"

Toria sympathized, but she said, "Not a good idea. This is the sort of party where you retire to a lounge when your feet hurt, but you run the risk of being held hostage by some older man who wants to talk about the economy with you while he blows cigar smoke in your face. Slip your shoes off under your gown. No one will notice if you shrink a few inches for a moment."

"And that's why you are worth every penny." Zhinu sighed in palpable relief as her feet flattened on the wooden floor. "Is this the sort of assistance you provide all your clients?"

"Only the ones we like. Where did Rob vanish to?"

Though they bore no responsibility for the werewolf's safety or location, Kane had an immediate answer. "Saw him wander off with a few gentlemen. Both of you tired of dancing?"

"And Rob wanted a stiffer drink," Zhinu said.

"You should have gone with him. Or found other ladies to accompany instead of hanging out with the help," Toria said. They also held no control over the client's actions, outside of her safety, but Zhinu would not mind the advice.

"You're not the help," Zhinu said, dismissing Toria's concern out of hand. She used Toria's arm as a brace while she slipped her high heels back on and regained her previous height. "You're practically family."

Even with Zhinu in heels, Toria and Kane made eye contact over her elaborate hairstyle. Kane pushed concern and worry through their link, and Toria returned a sense of agreement.

They were here to protect Zhinu, not launch her into society. That bit fell to the Wallace family.

But as she said, they were practically family.

"Family doesn't have to put up with this," Toria said. "Your draw."

The spread of cards Kane clutched offered no hopeful options. Even with their mental link locked down, Toria could not help the slight quirk of her upper lip that meant she had a potential win. He discarded the entire hand and redrew. His new cards provided no better luck, so he put off Toria's success and said, "Family would be caught up in that oh-so-polite conversation. Or at least, you would be. I wouldn't even be invited."

Zhinu's sheer boredom was palpable to those familiar with her, even from the distance where Toria and Kane perched on a low garden wall outside the picnic area. The women who surrounded her sipped tea and ate dainty sandwiches. They sat too far away to overhear the conversation. Still, from how little Zhinu participated, Kane suspected yet another round of gossip about people in Londinium the weredragon did not yet know.

The mercenaries had retreated to the edge of the gathering, thankful the maids who laid out the tea provided them with sandwiches and a large bottle of juice to share. It came in handy under the bright spring sun since they did not benefit from a pavilion to provide shade.

"Two pairs," Toria said, spreading her hand between them. "And incoming."

Saved by the cranky weredragon. Kane collected their cards and shuffled them into the deck. They both rose to greet Zhinu. She showed minor difficulty in storming across the grass in yet another pair of heels but managed it through the fury that flashed in her expression. "Are you okay?" Kane asked. He shoved the cards in his pocket and spread his feet.

But none of the women moved to follow Zhinu, staring after her with expressions ranging from disdain to bemusement.

"We're leaving." Zhinu's fingers tightened into the shape of claws at her sides. "Now." Her tone brooked no argument, even if they had been in a position to dictate her presence at an afternoon tea.

"I'll get the car." Toria cut across the grass toward the park entrance, giving the picnic area a wide berth.

Kane offered his elbow to Zhinu, and she unclenched one hand to accept it. They followed Toria at a more sedate pace. "What happened?" Zhinu might not confide in him. He wasn't Toria and did not have the same familiarity with their client. But at least she would know that Kane could lend a kind ear if needed.

She inhaled as if about to speak, but shut her mouth with a snap of teeth. Her pace quickened.

Kane escorted her away from the picnic, the weight of lupine stares between his shoulder blades like an itch he couldn't scratch.

Another evening, another ball. Tomorrow would be a day of quiet for Londinium's upper-classes, before Queen Moira called the full Parliament to session the following morning. Tonight's last hurrah marked an unofficial hiatus from the never-ending work of politics that extended long beyond the parliamentary season.

The ballroom in this manor house featured benches along the surrounding walls, at least. Toria sat with Kane in relative comfort while Zhinu danced with her husband.

"Hey, did Zhinu ever tell you why we left in such a rush yesterday?" Kane sipped water as he watched their charge.

The theme of this ball was springtime. Toria hated the lace that edged tonight's blouse, where it itched at her neckline, but her partner's darker skin set off the traditional navy pinstripe of his suit to elegant effect. In moments like these, Kane evoked his forefather Kojo, memories Toria shied away from because they often accompanied memories of death from her time in Nacostina.

She had put off answering long enough that Kane stopped watching Zhinu and turned to her instead. "Toria?"

No way out but through. "Zhinu is used to a court system built on meritocracy, where she was the anomaly elevated based on her bloodline." An older couple settled onto the bench to Kane's other side, so Toria lowered her voice to finish. "Zhinu is not used to women who were born to power and have no better use for it than to talk about who is sleeping with whom."

Her partner was better at people than she was, and he zeroed in on the direct quote portion of her response. "Let me guess. Rob is going to find his heir elsewhere?"

The Wallace clan had accepted the plan for Rob's title to pass to the eldest child of his sister, no matter the gender, since Rob's pairing with Zhinu would not produce children. Toria scratched the side of her neck until Kane captured her hand with his. "That was part of it," Toria said, "But it got worse."

Her partner had the patience of an oak tree, the picture of unmoving calm, even as curiosity flowed through their mental bond.

Toria tightened her hand on his. "The ladies at the tea asked which of us Zhinu was sleeping with."

"Why have us around, otherwise?"

"Exactly."

Never mind that bodyguards were a longtime tradition among the non-lupine elite of British society, a holdover from when human members of the peerage could identify a champion to represent them in a challenge for power. Other bodyguards accompanied the evening's attendants, Mercenary Guildmembers and otherwise. Nothing about their presence as Zhinu's escorts should have caused comment, except when young ladies practiced the age-old game of bitchiness for bitchiness's sake.

"Poor girl," Kane said. "She needs to make friends of her own station, and soon."

"She misses Oxenafor, where people judged her on her intelligence for the first time in her life. This is a replay of life in Qin, where she existed to be the artful extension of a man."

"And I'm sure the time spent in our presence at these formal events instead of with Rob does not—" Kane's voice broke off when the live musicians finished with a flourish, and they joined in the applause. Then, he huffed. "Damn it."

Rob disappeared among the swirling crowd, but Zhinu retreated from the dance floor to sink onto the bench on Toria's other side. "Still love dancing. Still hate shoes."

Toria made no outward acknowledgement of the negative mental tendril Kane slipped her way. She already agreed with him that this was not the time to raise their concerns. Instead, she asked, "Can I fetch you a drink?"

"Not your job. You know that. But a drink does sound lovely." Zhinu levered herself to her feet with a hand on Toria's shoulder and an accompanying groan of mock pain. "Help me get coffee, Kane."

With his hand caught by the weredragon, Kane had no choice but to follow Zhinu into the crowd. His frustration with Zhinu swept into Toria's brain, loud and clear, echoing her own.

Zhinu's actions would do nothing to clear the gossip. Toria gripped the edge of the bench in frustration, following Kane's tall form as it bobbed through the crowd and vanished in the direction of the buffet spread. As the room cleared out, other dancers having the same plan for refreshment during the musicians' break, a cluster of young women in an opposite corner caught her notice.

The three women stared at Toria as one, and for a moment, it was as if three large wolves peered through the trees. Giant predators who stalked their prey, chasing until it tired before circling to attack.

Toria stared back, lifting her chin and squaring her shoulders. Pampered ladies would not intimidate her when she had faced more immediate threats to her life.

One of the ladies redirected her attention. Then another. Finally, a quartet of laughing gentlemen broke Toria's line of sight with the last woman.

Londinium was a modern city built on the bones of an ancient one, and getting out of town into the open space of the surrounding countryside brought much-needed fresh air. Kane drove the electric town-car Rob had gifted his wife as a graduation present, a top-of-the-line model he'd itched to get his hands on. Though Zhinu was more than capable of driving the vehicle herself, she had urged Toria to join her in the backseat where they could relax in the open air with the top down while Kane put on bursts of speed along the highway.

Zhinu squealed as Kane took yet another turn in the country road at top speed, but Toria relaxed into the backseat with the knowledge that her partner was in perfect control. The air that rushed past them wasn't the gale of a windstorm, but the movement brought her contentment she could never find in an urban center.

The night before, once in their shared suite, Toria had agreed with her partner that they needed to speak with Zhinu about her public interactions with them. It would not be an easy conversation, but it was a necessary one. If Zhinu was to thrive in her new environment, she needed every tool and trick at her disposal. Toria meant to see her friend be a success in the long run, even if it required tough love.

But not now. Not with the wind in their hair, and a different sort of appointment on Zhinu's social calendar for the day.

Kane slowed as they encountered a turn-off on the road, marked by a sign that read "Foundry Laboratories." Zhinu fumbled in her purse for a paper that she passed forward to him as they neared a gatehouse that blocked the drive to a series of unassuming, slate-topped buildings. Two silos towered behind them, without any identifying marks as to their purpose. An armed guard exited the gatehouse as the town-car slowed to a stop before an open gate.

"Good afternoon," Kane said. "Lady Zhinu Wallace has an appointment with Dr. Meredith Tierney this morning." He handed the paper to the well-built security officer.

The man skimmed the contents and examined the women in the backseat. His attention slid past Zhinu, and he sketched a bow to Toria. "Lady Zhinu. It's a pleasure to have you here at the lab."

Toria froze, but Zhinu responded as if the man had addressed her. "Thank you, officer. It's a pleasure to be here."

The man flushed but recovered at once, shifting to Zhinu and repeating the bow. Toria gave him mental points when he did not make excuses for his mistake. "We hope you enjoy your visit."

He stepped to the front of the vehicle and said to Kane, "Please proceed to the first building. You can park in any of the empty spaces out front, and the security officer at the front desk will check you in."

When the man returned to the guardhouse and raised the gate, Kane followed his instructions. High-security fencing surrounded the property, and a maintained drive through short-clipped grass led to a cluster of buildings. The outside shared no hint of the work conducted inside, no clues as to what research the company performed.

Toria had refreshed her memory on the file concerning Meredith Tierney the night before. She looked forward to the meeting, even though her job was to fade into the background while Zhinu learned about this particular Wallace family holding. Eventually, Zhinu would assist Rob in managing the financial empire, and it was in her best interest to learn each small cog in the giant network. She might have completed a graduate degree from Oxenafor in history, but she had also studied economics and international relations to prepare for this role in her husband's life.

On the other hand, Toria's studies in metallurgy and chemistry during her time at Jarimis University gave her a genuine interest in the technological aspect of this laboratory's work. She was happy to accommodate Zhinu's request to ask questions of her own during the meeting with Tierney.

The brief biography on Tierney provided by Rob's secretary listed the woman as fifty-seven years old. Foundry Labs had employed her for almost ten years, and she had risen through the ranks to lead of the science division upon her predecessor's retirement a few months ago. Her listed specialties included mechanical engineering and aerospace propulsion, with the latter an unexpected focus in the era after the Last War.

But based on Toria's discovery with the radio back home, the world spell had fallen at last. This anonymous campus could conduct any sort of research.

A woman in a white lab coat entered the lobby from a rear door as Zhinu, Kane, and Toria finished pinning on visitor's badges. Toria recognized Tierney from the photo attached to her bio, and the stout woman approached Zhinu and extended her hand at once.

"Lady Wallace. I'm Dr. Meredith Tierney, the manager of the labs here. It's a pleasure to have you visit us today." The woman's politeness did not meet her eyes, the lines at the corners from age instead of good humor. Toria knew the type, a woman with pale skin from too much time spent inside. Her thinly disguised displeasure likely stemmed from irritation at the interruption to her work rather than at their presence.

"I'm excited to learn about what you do here." Zhinu grasped Tierney's hand in both of her own in a warm greeting. "Thank you for taking the time to meet with me today. I understand that you must be in the middle of many projects, but I do hope you'll indulge me with the full tour."

Once released from Zhinu's grasp, Tierney stuffed both hands in her coat pockets. "Of course, your ladyship. If you and your, ah, associates will please follow me." She gestured to the security officer behind the lobby's desk, and he pushed a button. A light next to the door Tierney had arrived from flipped from amber to green, and Tierney pushed it open. She held the door open for Toria to pass through, with Zhinu and Kane at her heels.

Instead of a bustling space where researchers rushed around and worked on multiple projects, a bare hallway dotted with occasional doors greeted them. When the door clicked shut behind them, Tierney said, "This building houses administrative offices. Accounting, payroll, and such. Were you interested in speaking to Ms. Sloane, our director of finances?"

"No, thank you," Zhinu said. "All of the laboratory's financial information is available to me in the city. I'm here to see what you do in practice, so the money side of things will make more sense when I review it later."

Tierney's thin lips paled further as her face tightened. But she made no response except to say, "Please follow me to the next building."

They traveled the length of the hall and through another security door activated with a swipe of the badge Tierney pulled from her pocket. Covered walkways led in three directions to other buildings, each with the same unassuming neutral siding. Tierney chose the left path, and when they entered the next building, mechanical delights assaulted Toria's senses.

This time, a large workspace dominated the area. Sparks flew in a distant corner as a welder, swathed in protective gear, joined two pieces of metal. Closer to the doorway, three scientists in lab coats that matched Tierney's gesticulated in conversation near a chalkboard covered in mathematical symbols. The nearest man stopped talking when he noted Tierney, which seemed to echo through the room in ripples that even silenced the welder.

Tierney gestured to Zhinu and said, "Lady Wallace wishes to learn about our work here. Please tell her about any current projects." She provided no further directions, and the silence continued through the lab for another few beats.

Soon, one of the nearby scientists stepped forward and favored Zhinu with a slight bow. "Lady Wallace, I'm Dr. Minke. I'd love to show you my current work on electric vehicles."

Like a flipped switch, the noise resumed throughout the lab. Tierney dropped back as Zhinu admired Dr. Minke's blueprints for an improved vehicle charging system, and the woman lost a bit of the tension in her shoulders after escaping Zhinu's attention. Though this piqued Toria's curiosity, the work Dr. Minke showed Zhinu soon captured her full attention.

"We've been developing these as supplemental military transports for a few years now," Dr. Minke said, leading them away from the two-dimensional blueprints and closer to life-size models in another section of the lab space. The lanky scientist, wearing casual clothing under his lab coat, accepted a handheld control system from an assistant and flipped a corner switch.

Zhinu yelped in glee when a robot moved, but Toria had anticipated the action. The four-legged machine shifted the blocky metal housing that contained its electronic brains, a clumsy mass of edges. Dr. Minke manipulated other switches on his controller, and the machine lifted its legs until it managed a jerky gait toward Zhinu.

External apprehension and disgust oozed through Toria's hindbrain, but she was not the source. From their place behind Zhinu, Toria placed two fingers against Kane's wrist and used the physical touch to enhance the reassurance she sent his way. "I know, they're creepy as all get out," she said. "But aren't they cool?"

Thin, jointed metal legs supported a metal body in a shape that evoked the skeletal structure of an over-sized wolf, but the noise as it moved came from whirring gears and pressurized hydraulics, not the click of nails against the cement floor. The lack of any facial attributes, or any head at all, added to the eeriness, but Toria laughed along with Zhinu as Dr. Minke prompted the robot to dance in place.

"I'm caught between terror and sheer delight," Zhinu said, once Dr. Minke powered down the robotic wolf. "Please, tell me the purpose of such a machine."

Toria tuned out the scientist's explanation because she already knew why the strange contraption existed. She had assisted the developers of the original prototype during her years at Jarimis University. The mechanical beasts that stood before them now dwarfed the models she had welded together under robotics students' instruction. But the British military had put out the call for such mechanical assistance for their human and lupine forces, vehicles that would be able to cross terrain as well as wolves, while also carrying supplies.

Dr. Minke explained all this to Zhinu, with frequent interjections by his colleagues. Toria knelt to examine the model that had danced under the scientist's command. The compact frame used smaller battery cells than the version she helped craft in college, and its four-legged gait had a metronome-like quality to its pace. The rubberized feet intrigued her the most. If these scientists could modify the legs to reduce the sound, the robot would be almost silent when—

Toria twisted in place at Kane's mental signal, but the newcomer who entered the lab wore a white coat of her own. With Kane stationed by Zhinu, whose full attention remained on Dr. Minke and his robotic wonders, Toria drifted away from the model and the enthusiastic group.

Tierney and the scientist, a young woman with a golden hue to her skin and deference portrayed by her very stance, conversed in whispers. Dr. Minke now dominated the novelty of the visiting nobility, and Toria could not pick out their low conversation under the electric pulse of the welder who had resumed work in the far corner. Despite her short stature, Tierney managed to loom over the petite scientist, who further hunched her shoulders. Her coat seemed dingy under the brilliant workspace lights compared to Tierney's bleached white, but the black headscarf that hid the woman's hair stood out more. Toria pushed unfulfilled curiosity through her link to Kane in answer to his mental tap. She had not seen a woman covering her hair since the time they spent in the eastern reaches of Roman territory three years ago with Asaron.

Tierney pointed to the far door, and the woman turned to leave. But her presence had not gone unnoticed by more than the warrior-mage pair.

With a quick apology, Zhinu broke away from the cluster of scientists. She cut a path between the robotic models, angling away from Toria and Kane before either of them could stop her. "Wait!"

The woman who had spoken with Tierney froze in her tracks. Toria neared the pair as Zhinu burst into a string of Qin. Though the tonal language meant nothing to Toria's ears, a palpable delight suffused her words.

But the woman said, "I'm sorry, Lady Wallace. I do not speak Qin."

"Oh!" Zhinu said. "My apologies. I assumed—"

Tierney brushed past Toria. "Excuse me. I need Ms. Khan to complete her errand for me. Shall we continue the tour?"

The other woman backed away. "I'm sorry, your ladyship. I really must go." She scurried from the room, ducking out a door that slammed closed behind her.

Zhinu turned to Toria, but Tierney stepped close to distract her. "I'm so glad you enjoyed this look at Dr. Minke's project," Tierney said. She was all smiles now, in contrast to how she spoke to the other woman and even to the way she previously acted as though Zhinu offered such a great imposition when they first arrived.

Toria tensed when Tierney clasped Zhinu's arm like they were friends.

"Yes, thank you. It was fascinating," Zhinu said. As if the interlude had never happened, her attention settled on Tierney. "Please, I look forward to seeing what other work you do here."

A different cast settled on Zhinu's curiosity as they left the space, through another covered passageway and into one of the tall silos on the property. As if she searched for something, not followed as a passive observer on this tour of a small part of the massive empire into which she had married.

Of course, the woman. Toria and Kane followed as Tierney spoke of lucrative military contracts. It was natural for Zhinu to gravitate toward someone who reminded her of home, a woman whose skin color marked her as from the Qin empire that dominated the lands east of Europa. But the woman did not speak Qin, and the accent of what little she said marked her as a British native. Even after the years Zhinu had spent in Oxenafor, her own Loquella accent still carried the bland vowels that marked her original teachers of the language as Roman.

All thoughts of the mysterious Ms. Khan evaporated from Toria's mind as they entered the silo at the foot of a rocket that towered above them.

Kane whispered out of the side of his mouth, for Toria's ears alone. "I guess this answers the question about whether the British have figured out all tech is back."

She ignored him, distracted by the clean lines of the rocket. Compared with the bumbling robotic dogs, this vehicle was a majestic bird. The Wallace family sigil decorated one side, and Toria circled the base, noting the nine engines that emerged from the bottom of the carbon-composite column. The opposite side sported the laboratory logo, accompanied by, she presumed, the names and brands of other financial sponsors.

Also, shorter than she first thought, about four stories high. But the silo could obviously accommodate even taller rockets. Like the ones intended to launch the missile she and Kane had been frantic to disarm in Limani, under the power of a tattooed mage, the man Kane had so ached to kill as he stripped the flesh from his leg to sever his link to the weapon—

Toria raised mental shields even as her mind sought Kane's to push reassurance and peace through their link. His hand tightened around hers, and she was once again alone in her mind.

But their link was a two-way street, and the aching emptiness pained her more than Kane's terrifying, visceral memories of a battle before their time as full mercenaries. She breathed with him, in through her nose and out through her mouth. Over and over, until his familiar presence tapped at her shields. When she dropped them, love and gratitude flooded the emptiness, washing it away with the power of a storm surge.

All the while, Zhinu and Tierney chatted about the possibility of resuming the scientific advances in communication halted by the Last War. If either noted the irony of a British and Qin woman discussing advanced technology, they made no note. Once Toria reassured herself that their companions paid no attention to the quiet drama occurring behind them, she leaned into Kane's side. "I'm sorry. I'd forgotten."

Forgotten that while she fought tooth and nail to return to her partner's side during a painful separation, the opposing forces held Kane captive near a nuclear weapon. Used as a vampire's sole food source and forced to sense the weapon's toxicity seep into the earth that provided his power. Before memories could overwhelm Toria again, Kane clamped them off from his end. "I don't think I ever will. Without warning, this was—" With his free arm, he encompassed the gleaming skin of the rocket, so innocuous despite the power it must contain. "Too much."

"I suppose that must be what my anxiety attacks feel like to you."

In their relative privacy, Kane pressed his face to the top of Toria's head for a moment. "I'm not sure that memory has the same power as fear. Either way, I'll be happy to be away from this thing. But I know you're intrigued. Go play."

With her partner's blessing, Toria joined the edge of Tierney's conversation with Zhinu. She had perfected the art of hiding curiosity beneath a guise of impassivity, the inconsequential bodyguard, ages ago.

But Zhinu knew well her bodyguard's academic interests. She angled her body to absorb Toria into the conversation, asking, "Toria, did you know that the British have been using high-altitude balloons to test the limits of long-range communication without the help of elven enchantments since after the Last War?"

"I knew something of the sort." Toria also knew the Romans had been affecting similar workarounds to the elven limits on technology for the same amount of time. She assumed that the Qin had also performed research along the same lines. And now that the world spell had fallen, research on all sides would ramp up.

"The next step," Tierney said, "is turning former weapons technology to peacetime exploits. This rocket will carry a payload higher than any weather balloon."

Toria received Kane's mental warning of someone on approach a moment before a low throat-clearing captured Tierney's attention. The group turned to the newcomer as one.

Tierney's mood soured as she spotted the woman who had interrupted them before. She crossed the space to grab the woman's arm and tug her out of sight around a bank of machinery.

Abandoned mid-conversation, Zhinu and Toria drifted toward where Kane lurked near the silo's entrance. "What is that about, do you suppose?" Toria asked.

Zhinu tapped her chin with a blue fingernail. "It would be rude to eavesdrop."

"But you're doing it anyway, right?"

The weredragon, her senses as heightened as those of any werewolf or vampire, cocked one shoulder. "Well, it's hard not to." Zhinu's gaze unfocused as she dialed into her hearing. "And it's nothing important, anyway. Dr. Tierney is angry that Ms. Khan has not finished a project. Such interactions were typical among professors and their research assistants in Oxenafor, so I don't imagine the private sector would differ much from academia. It's strange, though—" Zhinu broke off as Tierney reappeared, sans her underling.

"My apologies for the continued interruptions," Dr. Tierney said. "We're behind my intended schedule, so shall we move on?"

42

Toria did not blame Zhinu for acquiescing to Tierney's request when Kane's stress faded from her mind as they left sight of the rocket.

Later, as Kane drove them back into the city and Zhinu jotted notes to herself about the excursion, a half-finished thought prompted Toria to ask, "What's strange?"

Zhinu's pen paused. "What?"

"Earlier, when you listened in on Tierney and her assistant. You said something was strange." Toria felt Kane's attention on them via the rearview mirror, listening to the exchange.

"A passing fancy at the time, I think. I wouldn't be able to tell you now." Zhinu returned to her note-taking, even with her evasiveness evident in the set of her shoulders.

Zhinu dismissed them upon their return to the townhouse. Not their official night off, per their contract, but Toria longed for a warm bath followed by time to read in bed. Unfortunately, a note from Rob waited in their suite. "We've been asked to dinner."

Kane froze while hanging his sword belt on the hook behind the door. "By whom?"

Amplified curiosity fluttered in Toria's mind like furious butterflies. "Rob invited us to join him and Zhinu tonight. Nothing fancy." In that awkward position as not quite staff yet not part of the family, despite their friendship with the lord and lady of the house, she and Kane often dined in their suite on trays brought from the kitchen. Neither minded eating the same fare as the well-treated household staff. Still, they did mind how Rob's driver ogled Toria and the housekeeper's frequent derisive comments about the "mercenary lifestyle." This compromise suited all.

Kane grinned, a wolfish expression that would not have been out of place on Rob. "That'll put Pierce's panties in a twist. Do we need to dress for this?"

The note had not specified, but better safe than sorry. The pair presented themselves in the dining room at the appointed time, showered but wearing personal clothing instead of the swanky garments Zhinu provided for her formal escort. Rob and Zhinu awaited them alone.

"Thank you for joining us tonight," Rob said as he pulled out Toria's chair for her to sit. "I realize this is beyond your purview, but it seems silly to miss out on time with actual friends when you're living in my house."

"What he means," Zhinu said after she thanked Kane for drawing out her chair, "is that Rob can't stand another moment with people he has to be political around, and you're a refreshing neutral party."

"The Season has barely begun, but I already crave an opinion that doesn't have a political motive behind it." Rob lifted his wine glass once the footman who'd poured for them left the dining room. "You might be under contract, but I hope you do understand that you wouldn't have the contract if I didn't trust you with Zhinu's—and my own—life. To friends."

They echoed the toast and drank as the footman returned with the first course. "We appreciate the job as much as we also consider you true friends, as well," Toria said. She ignored the mental equivalent of Kane kicking her under the table and asked, "But what makes you think we wouldn't have a political motive in discussion with you?"

Kane hid a cough in his napkin.

Zhinu said, "I told you, Robert."

"Perhaps political motive is a misnomer in this circumstance," Rob said. "All opinions are political in some regard. But the two of you present a broader perspective than most of my compatriot's views, which I value. And why I asked you to join us tonight."

With any other pair of clients, Toria and Kane would spend an exhausting evening playing conversational games. Avoiding expressing any opinions, political or otherwise, that might put further employment in jeopardy. Or their current work, contracted or not.

But Rob's toast before the meal had been sincere. These were their friends first. Toria and Kane would not let Zhinu come to harm regardless of whether Rob paid them for the effort. A poor method for a mercenary to make a living, but luckily, Rob understood their services' value and compensated them accordingly.

So, instead of responding to Rob right away, Toria stared across the table at

Kane. She tucked one of her feet against his, her low flat even with his loafer. Physical contact enhanced their mental link, even through clothing.

With the additional connection, the affirmation from Kane's side of their link became enhanced with overtones of truth and fondness. He supported openness with Rob and Zhinu but underneath sent a quiet line of query. A questioning sense that implied Kane would follow her lead, despite his feelings on the matter.

It was a rare occasion when she and Kane held contrary opinions on things that mattered. Toria broke the connection with Kane. "You're right," she told Rob. "Kane and I aren't British. We're not Qin or Roman either, which are the perspectives you're used to accommodating during political decision-making."

"We're from Limani," Kane said. "No one ever thinks of us."

Rob jabbed his spoon in Kane's direction. "My point exactly. No one ever seems to think of Limani except when your city stands in the way of something we need."

Slight apprehension curled around Toria's spine, but she didn't know whether to blame her chronic anxiety or a legitimate fear. "Why? Does Limani block Britannia now?" The words came out steady, despite the tremor in her hand that clutched her fork. She set the utensil down and pressed her fingers on the edge of the table.

"Not at the moment." Rob pushed away his empty appetizer plate. "But I received distressing news today. The formal announcement will be made during the opening of Parliament tomorrow, but my sources close to the queen wanted me aware of the situation due to my economic position and influence."

"News about Limani?" Toria asked. She also nudged her half-eaten salad away.

"No," Rob said. "I apologize. I'm going about this in circles. I use your home as an example of your different perspectives on things. But now I seek your counsel from a different position you hold. There are mercenaries aplenty in Britannia these days. But there are far fewer mages. And I cannot let the potential information resource I have in the two of you go to waste."

Toria wasn't sure what direction Rob led with this conversation. "Right. Not many people in this land have a personal connection with mages—much less warrior-mages."

"How can we help?" Kane asked.

"British intelligence has reason to believe that the world spell cast by the elves after the Last War is no more. That there are no more limits on technology," Rob said. "But since I am not privy to how they might have discovered this fact, I wanted to ask the two of you whether this was something you could sense, as mages."

Blood roared in Toria's ears, and across the table, Kane froze in the act of reaching for his water. Just for a beat, and then he continued the movement as if he'd never been startled.

But their dining companions consisted of a werewolf and a weredragon. Rob and Zhinu would note Kane's hesitation, and the frantic beating of Toria's heart would be as loud to them as her normal speaking voice.

There was no denying Rob's question.

Even after his fortifying sip of water, Kane waved for Toria to take the lead on this one. She was the one who stayed awake so many late nights, arguing magical theory with Archer or Liam or Syri or combinations of the three. About time travel and shadows and blood. About the primal magic she could touch through her connection with storm, while Kane's affinity with earth was a hundred percent elemental.

She clenched her jaw, though she had no reason to lie. No reason to hide their knowledge. "Yes," she said. "We know that the world spell is broken."

Would Rob press for more information? Ask how long the spell had been down? Ask whether they had a role in its fall? Because Toria was in no frame of mind to revisit those memories.

Instead, all Rob said was, "I see. Thank you for confirming that fact for me."

Zhinu's lack of exclamation at Rob's initial question meant he must have broken the news to her previously. "Unfortunately, I don't know as much about what this means for the world as I wish I did. Is this why those robotic creatures worked?" she asked.

"Among other things." Toria flexed her fingers to promote blood flow and stop them from tingling. "That tall, fancy rocket Dr. Tierney showed us today wouldn't have a chance of working if the spell was still active."

"Yes, I rather thought the projects coming from the laboratory were too optimistic," Rob said. "But as long as they continued under budget, the benefits seemed to outweigh the risks."

"That's why you wanted Zhinu to tour the lab today, isn't it?" Kane asked. "Not so Zhinu would see the tech in development there, but so that we would?"

"Correct," Rob said. "Apologies for my deception, my love."

"Think nothing of it. I still found the experience fascinating," Zhinu said.

A footman appeared to collect their plates, and another served the main course, bringing a temporary halt to the conversation. But it also gifted Toria a few much-needed moments to collect herself and consider their next moves. "But you wanted more than a confirmation from us?" Though the roast's aroma tantalized her taste buds, eating felt out of the question with her roiling stomach's current state.

"You've caught me out," Rob said. His eyes flickered golden for a split second as he chewed his first bite of beef, but the man who spoke after swallowing was more civilized human than hungry wolf. "This development changes many things on a global scale."

"And now we're in my purview," Zhinu said. "Tensions with my people—with the Qin—have been stable for a few years. But population expansion has been growing on the continent. Tensions with Roma are higher now, aren't they?" It was not a real question. The woman held an advanced degree in international relations, despite her frequent jokes about attending the classes to prepare her for her eventual marriage.

"We're not yet at cold war status," Rob said. "But we have to assume the Romans are also aware the world spell is no longer active."

Yet another piece of information Toria had no reason to hide from Rob. "I can guarantee it. The vampires played a role in the activation of the spell itself."

Rob paused. "I see."

"Not going to ask how we know that?" Kane asked.

"I imagine I've taken advantage of our friendship enough for tonight," Rob said. "But in reality, the history of the world spell has never been my interest. The effect it had on the world is."

"Dr. Tierney impressed upon me that the technology the lab worked on was all in the name of increasing communications abilities," Zhinu said. "Even the military contracts maintained by the robotics department are in a support capacity."

"But we do not run the only technology development in the empire." Rob's meal lay forgotten, a lone bite of roast cooling on the end of his fork. "Other labs could be working on combat technology. The *military* is definitely working on combat technology."

"How do we find out whether this is happening?" Zhinu asked.

"In our country? I can go back to my contacts and make some inquiries," Rob said.

Toria pushed a carrot around her plate. "I suppose we have to assume that if the Romans are aware of the world spell falling, they've stepped up their technological development as well."

"But there's no reason to," Zhinu said. Though the rest sat still, she continued to eat with mechanical motions. "No one is at war."

Kane's ashen fingers gripped his now-empty water glass. "There's always the potential for war."

"How true that is," Rob said. He stared across the table. Zhinu's eyes locked with his.

For a moment, they might have sat alone in the room. Nearly a century passed after the Last War ended before a marriage between the British and Qin empires. And even this marriage involved political manipulations that had seen Zhinu exiled from her homeland. Toria sat with the physical representation of how war could affect people even decades after it had nominally ended.

Kane drained half his water glass in one long sip. "Not much the four of us can do about it at the moment, I suppose."

"Right," Zhinu said. "Robert, your food is getting cold. Toria, my secretary told me you borrowed the first book in the new Henderson series from the library. How are you enjoying it so far?"

With the conversation shifted, the four returned to their meals. Magic shivered across Toria's skin, and when she bit into the carrot, it tasted fresh from the oven.

Kane winked over the table, and she responded to Zhinu's book question as if the world's fate had not shifted.

They did have the next night off, per contract. Once Zhinu assured Kane she would settle into the library for an evening of correspondence and reading, he demanded his partner accompany him to the nearest mercenary bar.

Toria roiled with anxiety hidden behind walls of humor, both genuine and sarcastic. She needed to blow off steam, and Kane needed to dull their connection with a drink or three while she did it.

The nearest merc bar sat far from the exclusive neighborhood where Rob and Zhinu maintained their Londinium household. Not their usual haunt in this city, but it featured the requisite retired mercs smoking outside the entrance and advertised that day's special as half-priced draft beer. Perfect.

Kane paid the taxi fare and led Toria across the street toward the entrance. The two battle-worn men outside the bar made no secret of examining them both.

Toria's magical presence vibrated under the men's attention. She had left her rapier behind, but a faint whiff of ozone drifted on the breeze. A natural spring storm brewed in the sky above the city, and if his partner wasn't careful, it'd open right on top of them.

He grabbed Toria's shoulder and propelled her into the bar, ignoring the mercs who let them pass without comment as they lit new cigarettes. "Get drinks," he said, figuring an immediate task would distract her. "I'll find seats."

They had worked out the perfect strategy over time. Kane's height and imposing form tended to clear space, making it easier for them to find a place to park for the evening. And though plenty of female mercenaries existed, Toria's youth and appearance often attracted prompter service from behind the bar.

When Toria reappeared at his side, clutching a pitcher of beer and two empty glasses, Kane had claimed a booth as it cleared out. She slid into the seat across from him and poured their drinks. They raised the glasses to absent friends, clinked them together, and downed the first swallows without a word.

"Oh, I needed this." Toria shifted on her side of the booth until she leaned against the wall and stretched her legs out on the bench.

A single light lit their table from above, casting the rest of the semi-crowded room in shadow. Humidity weighted the air that swirled in through the open door, mixing with the familiar bar scents of spilled beer and old leather from the booths that lined the walls. The chatter and laughter of mercenaries and assorted hangers-on enjoying an evening on the town surrounded them in a dull roar, highlighted with occasional cheers as the television above the bar broadcast a local rugby match.

Not a dancing sort of establishment. So tonight, they would drink together until a handsome enough man caught Toria's eye, and the two disappeared into the night. Kane would drink alone and admire the surrounding men from a tipsy distance while Toria relaxed more actively. When the bar closed, they would rendezvous at the Wallace townhouse and pass out curled together in one of their beds.

Kane refilled their drinks. Onlookers might find it odd that the pair drank together in silence. Those on the outside missed the undercurrent of constant communication that amplified as alcohol thinned the shields between them.

As those shields warped and faded, coalescing instead into a fluctuating sphere that encompassed both warrior-mages, the contentment-arousal-searching Kane expected from Toria was absent. Instead, contentment-longing-rue flowed into his mind.

He sat straight up. Beer sloshed over the side of his glass, but he paid it no mind. "It's that serious between you and Liam?"

Serious enough that Toria would not seek out a temporary bedmate this night. Perhaps not on any of the many more nights they spent under contract to Zhinu Wallace.

She did not react to his burst of movement, keeping her attention on the play of light through the amber liquid in her glass. "I guess? We kind of never talked about it."

"You never talked about it."

"Nope."

"You never talked about the status of your relationship before you left him behind in Limani for half a year."

Toria twisted on the bench to face Kane. "The guy waited for me for decades. I hated to bring up how I was about to leave him again."

"You don't even know what you are to each other?"

"Of course, I do!" She slammed her glass on the table, and the physical impact rippled like an echo through their link. "But like I said, he waited for me for decades, and he looks almost the same as the day I left Nacostina. He's going to outlive me by centuries. How can I ask him to devote himself to me when I'm going to grow old and die in a fraction of his life?"

Kane refilled their glasses and set the empty pitcher at the end of the table. "He moved in with you a few weeks ago."

"That was a logical financial arrangement."

"And you're going to be monogamous while on the other side of the planet?"

"Why not?" Toria picked at a cuticle. "You're monogamous with Archer."

"That's different," Kane said. "You've spent our entire adult lives hopping in and out of beds. I think I'm allowed to be curious when that stops."

The conversation paused when a passing waitress collected the empty pitcher. After she requested a refill, Toria turned to Kane. "There's nothing to be curious about. We're both capable of celibacy on a long-term contract." But this was their first long-term contract since Toria and Liam got together. And she hadn't sought sex elsewhere on their handful of small jobs since then, either.

A thread of anxiety-hesitation-fear wound through the dampening effects of the alcohol—time for Kane to back off. "I had no intention of questioning you," he said. "We had a routine."

"Routines change," Toria said. "Now, we get drunk together instead."

Kane circled his finger through the condensation that gathered on the scarred wooden table. They would get drunk together, get a taxi to the Wallace townhouse, and...what? Go to their separate beds?

The grand tradition of bonded mage pairs included romances that were the stuff of epics. Not all of them, but enough that Kane's lack of sexual attraction to the female form meant he and Toria bucked the trend. His relationship with

Archer had never interfered with their bond. The past few months Toria spent with Liam hadn't either.

But not wanting to have sex with each other did not mean their bond existed on the mental plane alone. Touch reinforced their connection as much as it strengthened it.

He did not want to spend the next few months with the occasional hug.

And, of course, with their shields so connected, Toria read all of this as if Kane's face was an open book.

"Hey, relax." Toria laced her hand with Kane's across the table. "I'm not kicking you out of my bed tonight. The entire routine won't change. I'm just saving cash on hotel rooms."

Kane held her hand tight. Everything Toria had felt before settled on him, and he absorbed the love-friendship-devotion she flooded his way. For a moment, the crowd faded away. As much as he loved Archer, Toria held half of his soul.

"You okay, love?"

Kane returned her flood of love with a deluge of affection. "Yes. Thank you. So, we're drinking and admiring men together?"

"Sounds like an excellent new routine."

The waitress had not yet returned with their fresh pitcher. And if they intended to get drunk together, they might as well do it right. "I'll order the shots." Kane slid out of the booth.

The crowd at the bar had grown, but he found an open space near the entrance. The evening had done little to ease the oppressiveness of the air outside. It would be a hell of a thunderstorm when it broke. If Toria wasn't getting laid tonight, no wonder his partner did not oppose dampening her senses with alcohol to avoid the temptation to meddle with the weather system.

He leaned against the bar, waiting for one of the busy bartenders to spare a moment for him. Kane hadn't pegged the two mercs outside as bouncers when they arrived, but the two men remained, smoking away.

Another man stood inside the front door, and if the evening's plan involved admiring attractive gentlemen, he was a decent offering. Denim hugged his hips, and Kane had no complaints that the T-shirt enveloping his torso appeared to have shrunk in the wash. Tattoos painted his bare arms, but the bar's dim lighting and the man's dusky skin made the details of the ink hard to make out.

A bronze stud pierced one earlobe. If the other side featured a matching decoration, Kane couldn't spot it under the mass of black hair that tumbled down the man's cheek, almost touching his shoulder. It would be so easy to nip that earlobe with gentle teeth, to bury his hands in that hair, find out whether it felt as soft as it appeared, and tilt the man's lips to his neck—

Except Kane stood taller than him. He checked over his shoulder, and yes, Toria stared at the same man. He shot a mental jab through their link. His partner jumped, but dared to smirk at him instead of signal any sort of embarrassment.

When he turned back, the man had left the wall. As he strolled out the bar's entrance, he shouldered past one of the smoking mercenaries.

"Hey!" The smoker dropped his cigarette. "Watch yourself, boy."

But Kane noted what the smoker did not. The tattooed man had slipped his wallet from the smoker's pocket and into his own. A deft move, and one Kane might have missed without Toria's attention on the man, amplifying his own.

When the man ignored the smoker, the older mercenary grabbed his elbow in a clawed grip. "Hey," he said again. "You wanna apologize?"

In most cases, Kane might have demanded the man return the wallet. He pushed away from the bar as the man shook off the smoker's grip. But when the man turned, the second smoker blocked his path.

He loomed over the tattooed man. "My friend wants an apology."

A shimmer of magic blurred the tattooed man's silhouette for a split second, and power licked at Kane's skin. Neither of the smokers reacted, but that amount of energy made the hair on Kane's scalp raise.

No way had his partner missed that pull of energy, so he pushed reassurance in Toria's direction as he exited the bar. Kane slung one arm over the tattooed man's shoulders and offered a tight smile to the old merc. "Sorry about that. My friend's had too much to drink. We'll be on our way."

He dug his fingers into the man's upper arm, ignoring the softness of his shirt and skin in favor of a snap of power. The pickpocket caught on at once, allowing Kane to drag him away from the bar without protest.

Once the men passed two storefronts, Kane released him. But the man didn't step away, and this close, reflections from the streetlight glowed amber in his eyes. He was no werewolf, though, not with the magical energy that continued to coalesce around them. Kane pressed his index finger to the man's sternum and shunted the excess power into the ground. When he did this trick with Toria, it felt like manipulating his personal power. Even with Archer, the power flowed through him like liquid, like the water of Archer's affinity. Now, though, the energy dragged through his skin, leaving his insides scraped raw as it dissipated into the earth. Kane grit his teeth and suppressed a grunt of pain.

The tattooed man crossed his arms, muscles bulging with tension. "What the hell did you do that for?"

Kane ignored the question. "I've never experienced magic like that before."

"And you never will again." A scowl darkened the man's face. He brushed past Kane and crossed the street, ambling into a crowd and never appearing out the other side. A trick as deft as palming that wallet.

When Kane returned to their booth at the bar, Toria nursed a fresh beer. A full pitcher and four shot glasses sat on the table. Two of the shot glasses were already empty.

Toria nudged the full ones toward Kane. "You're already behind. And when I said admiring men, I didn't mean chasing them out into the street."

"I saw him lift a wallet." Kane tipped back a shot. The vodka burned less than the man's strange magic.

"It's such a shame when the cute ones turn out to be jerks."

Except Kane had not demanded that the mage return the wallet. The unfamiliar magic had shaken him, distracted him. He downed the second shot and chased it with a sip of beer. "Yeah. A shame."

"It's official. We're too old for hard liquor." Toria wished she had swallowed another dose of painkillers before the evening's formal event. She squinted at the strings of lights that echoed the decorations in the main ballroom. Did the dots in her vision reflect from the bright decor or within her aching skull?

Kane stood tall next to her, the picture of utter relaxation. He never had hangovers. Something about the healing gifts that earth magic gave him. Absolutely, completely unfair. "Somewhere, Asaron is laughing, and he doesn't know why," Kane said. "Also, may I remind you the shots were your idea."

Toria ignored the barb because her partner was right on both accounts. Asaron, a vampire in their extended family, approached two millennia in age. He had done his best to teach the teenagers he helped raise to hold their liquor, but the bounds of the human constitution limited them.

Zhinu had shown pity on Toria after mocking her on the drive through the city. While the formal estate owned by the queen's brother in Londinium held a large room for dancing, Zhinu confined herself to a smaller side room to trade conversation with other ladies. Toria could better handle the room's brightness and the murmur of speech than brightness *and* music.

Proving once again that Zhinu was the best client ever, she broke away from her companions with a brief apology and brought Toria her glass of water. "I'm sorry the ice has melted," Zhinu said. "But Lady Jillian corralled me into a stupid debate about hemlines, and I couldn't figure out how to get away."

"You realize that fetching your bodyguard drinks is not how things are done, right?" But Toria accepted the glass and drained half the contents. She wanted to press the cold glass to her aching forehead, but professionalism won out.

"Mocking another woman for wearing the same evening gown twice in one season also should not be how things are done, but tell that to those oh-so-proper ladies." Zhinu scanned the room but did not seem to find who she sought. "Kane, please escort me to find Lady Norinne because it seems she's acquired a new friend who wants to compliment her on her gown. I imagine Toria should patrol the garden perimeter and check security."

Toria could kiss Zhinu, even as the weredragon dragged Kane away without a backward glance. With so many high-level royals in attendance at this ball, the estate featured more security than most places in the British Empire. But a stroll through the gardens, dim and quiet at this evening hour, would be a relief.

Kane could poke her through their link if he needed her, so Toria wasted no time depositing her empty glass on a side table and fleeing the crowded room.

Stepping outside onto a patio, vacant but for a flirting couple in one corner, induced an immediate improvement to her spirits. The air had lost the humidity from the previous evening since the storm had broken soon after Toria and Kane returned to the townhouse. She'd had nothing to do with the shift in weather, despite Kane's inebriated teasing that turned into a full-blown tickle fight as they tumbled into her bed.

Toria paused as she stepped onto a gravel pathway. Perhaps evidence that the pair used only one of the suite's beds last night would prompt gossip through the household staff, and Rob's driver would cease his ham-handed attempts at wooing her.

She drifted along the path. It was too dark to give the manicured formal garden her proper appreciation, not that she had Kane's knowledge of plants. The lack of lighting and her urge to stay near the house meant Toria followed the path around the mansion, toward the front entrance where luxury town-cars streamed in an endless parade to drop off and retrieve guests.

Flashing red and blue lights marred the serenity of the evening. Toria expected paramedics due to the advanced age of some of the human partygoers. Instead, three marked police transports curved around the drive, pulling ahead of the waiting vehicles.

Lights, but no sirens. And with no sounds of alarm emanating from the mansion, it meant the police who emerged came for someone in the house, not in response to an emergency. Toria dropped her shields long enough to send a mental image of the arriving collection of uniformed and plainclothes officers to Kane, better information than a general impression could provide, and increased her pace toward the front of the house.

She kept to the shadows because even though she had nothing to hide, a surreptitious watcher had a better chance of gathering information than an unknown woman who stumbled into an operation in progress. And this was not a social call, as one of the plainclothes officers flashed a badge to the estate staff who handled the door. Toria did not pick out all of the words, but heard the unmistakable tone of orders given.

The woman who had accepted Zhinu's invitation at the door, who had offered Toria and Kane a warm welcome instead of treating them as invisible staff, backed away from the entrance to let the police pass. In the foyer's golden light, her face grew ashen next to a uniformed officer as the rest of the police poured into the building.

Kane pulsed assent through their link, acknowledging Toria's message. But the tail end of his signal switched to a flash of panic and his shields crashed shut, cutting off their connection.

Toria sprinted off the path, across the lawn. A police officer snatched at her arm as she passed, but she dodged him and slipped through the door. Easy enough to disappear into the curious mass who crowded the foyer to view the unfolding drama.

Her link with Kane drew her through the collection of nobility and other guests. She cut through men and women alike, ignoring the curses and gasps in her wake. Out of the foyer, down a hallway, across a parlor, and into the ballroom.

She pushed between two men into the grand room. Instead of music, voices raised in furious argument dominated the space. The police circled a trio in the center of the ballroom like crows cutting parrots away from their flock. She found her partner and clients trapped within the cluster of tense police. Zhinu stood between Kane and Rob, and all three glared at the ball's uninvited guests.

As Toria crossed the open space that demarcated the spectacle, Zhinu spotted her. The noblewoman ducked between two of the police and threw herself into Toria's arms. Hands reached for weapons, and Toria thrust the woman behind her. She raised one hand and caught the line of energy from Kane. With fingers splayed, electricity crackled through the room.

Toria had no desire to knock a dozen police unconscious. But the client came first. "Zhinu?" She left any specific question unspoken, but the other woman would fill in the blanks. Did Zhinu need Toria and Kane to extract her from this situation? Toria had no idea why Londinium police had come for Zhinu, but that was not her current priority.

"It's okay," Zhinu said. Her voice caught on the words, and she swallowed. To the police, she said, "I will come with you as long as my bodyguard Toria Connor accompanies me."

One of the uniforms whispered into the ear of a plainclothes officer. Both of them studied Toria, and she lowered her extended hand. Kane absorbed the magic and grounded it, but the scent of ozone lingered in the air. She kept her other arm tucked around Zhinu.

The plainclothes officer, an older detective in a suit purchased ten pounds ago, inched closer to Toria and Zhinu. "That is highly irregular, ma'am."

A lupine growl emanated from Rob, so soft it was felt more than heard. "You will refer to my wife as 'your ladyship.' She is not a common criminal for you to scoop off the street, especially if you will not inform us of the charges."

Toria had seen Rob's wolf form before, but he had never terrified her more than at this moment. Zhinu was their priority, but Rob was their friend. If he shifted and attacked the police, should they stop him before he caused a greater mess? Toria did not even know what the current mess was.

"I'm sure his lordship would prefer not to cause further disruption." Sarcasm rolled off the detective's tongue.

"I'd prefer to understand why Londinium's finest feel the need to harass my wife." Rob snapped off the end of the sentence with bared teeth.

"Fine," the detective said. Silence fell across the ballroom as the mutters from onlookers faded away at once. The better for the gathered elite to learn about the brewing scandal involving Earl Wallace's foreign wife. With a gesture, as if the crowd proved his point, the detective continued, "Zhinu Wallace, you are under arrest for the murder of Sarnai Khan."

Kane would have preferred to be anywhere but this town-car. Palpable tension strung between Rob and the Wallace family lawyer, Sir Philip Exeter. Who Sir Exeter was most furious at was unclear, but the man had expressed his outrage in full volume when Rob and Kane arrived at his house.

Now, Kane sat in Rob's sophisticated town-car's front seat while the two men glowered in the rear seat. At least the lawyer was not a werewolf. If the gaze pricking the back of his neck had been supernatural, it would not have been tenable.

Rob's driver slipped through the streets of Londinium, clear of traffic at this late hour. Detective Crouse had informed them that the police would remand

Zhinu into custody at the main headquarters for Londinium's police. No mere local precinct for the wife of a nobleman.

Sir Exeter shattered the silence with his gravel-filled voice. "Tell me again what they accused your wife of."

"Murder, of all things!" Anxiety rent Rob's words. "Said she killed a laboratory technician at one of the Wallace holdings."

"Has her ladyship ever even met this supposed victim?"

"I don't—"

"Yes," Kane said. "We encountered her twice during our visit to Foundry Laboratories a few days ago. Lady Wallace had a brief exchange of words the first time, but not the second. She was never alone with Ms. Khan."

"Well, that's something, at least. Thank you, Mr. Nalason."

Kane did not correct the lawyer's butchering of his surname. They had more significant problems at the moment. His connection with Toria strengthened as they approached Londinium's government district, and anger-frustration-worry from his partner added to his mental burden. He tightened his grip on the door handle, even as he pushed reassurance to Toria of their close approach.

The driver left them at the main entrance, and Kane escorted Rob and Sir Exeter into the building. The officers on duty balked at allowing a second professional mercenary on the premises. Without pause, Rob insisted Kane accompany them as his personal protection.

The might of a werewolf nobleman whose eyes burned under the overhead fluorescent lamp, who seemed to invite the chance to shift at the slightest insult, proved above the desk sergeant's pay grade.

Kane divested himself of the knives concealed under his suit without protest. No physical wards brushed his shields when they entered the building, which meant the city police had no mages on staff. He and Toria carried physical weapons as a symbol of their chosen profession, but he was still one of the most dangerous people in the building without them.

Another officer led the trio up an elevator and through a maze of corridors to a small, windowless room. Rob wrapped Zhinu in his arms as soon as they entered. Kane joined Toria at the far wall.

"I will speak to the detective in charge," Sir Exeter said after Zhinu left Rob's embrace and greeted him. "I trust you have not said anything to your disadvantage since your arrest?"

Though the lawyer was no werewolf, Zhinu kept her gaze downcast in respect. "No, sir."

"Good. Keep it that way." He knocked on the door, then slipped out when it opened.

"What the hell is going on, Zhinu?" With a gentle push, Rob settled her into a chair. He turned a second to sit facing his wife and reclaimed her hands.

"I don't know! I barely spoke to the woman, and they're saying I murdered her!" Mascara streaked Zhinu's cheeks, evidence of her tears. She accepted Rob's handkerchief and dabbed at her damp face. "She was certainly alive when I saw her at the laboratory."

"And you haven't been alone since," Rob said. "You've either been at the house or with Toria and Kane."

Toria stiffened next to Kane at the statement, which sent the same rush of unease through him. What Rob said was untrue. Zhinu had been alone. While they had been out drinking the previous evening, Rob had gone out for a card game with friends. Zhinu's lady had the night off as well. They left Zhinu at the townhouse, but had no guarantee she stayed there. Ridiculous. Because that had nothing to do with the bigger question, this crazy notion that Zhinu had murdered a woman she had exchanged two sentences with.

Sir Exeter returned, trailing the detective who had interrupted the ball with such fanfare. Detective Crouse placed a folder on the table and settled into the chair across from Zhinu and Rob, sparing no glance for the mercenaries in the corner.

"Now that your lawyer is present," Crouse said, "are you ready to speak to me?"

After Exeter motioned his assent, Zhinu said, "Yes, though I have no idea why I'm a suspect in this crime."

Crouse placed his hand on the folder but did not flip it open. "Lady Wallace, I might not look like much, but I'm the detective responsible for crime at the highest level of society in this city. And that means werewolves." He dipped his chin in respect to Rob before his narrow-eyed attention returned to Zhinu.

"Well, there's your answer to this mess right there," Sir Exeter said. "Because Lady Wallace is assuredly not a werewolf." He huffed in exasperation and buttoned his coat as if his statement cleared everything up, and they should all return home at once.

"No, Lady Wallace is not a werewolf." Crouse lifted the top of the folder to reveal its contents to the room at large. "She is something quite different."

Toria sucked air between her teeth as the contents of Kane's stomach rearranged themselves. The folder held a blurry black and white image, a picture enlarged enough to lose its sharpness. But there was no mistaking what it showed. A sinuous creature the size of a horse, scales glinting under the summer sun, where Zhinu lounged on a large boulder. The picture did nothing to highlight her weredragon form's beauty, the shades of sapphire fading to azure across her flexible scales. Or the delicate ears that swept from the top of her head.

It did, however, show Zhinu's claws.

Rob slammed his hand on the table. "Where did you get this picture?"

"It's from two summers ago," Zhinu said, leaning forward to study the image. "In the countryside. I thought I'd be safe there."

"You were at the edge of a protected nature reserve," Crouse said. "This camera tracks wildlife, and you're lucky the naturalist who retrieved the footage gave it to his wife, an officer in Her Majesty's private intelligence force, instead of the tabloids."

Sir Exeter waved his hand over the picture. "How many people know about—*this?*"

Crouse leaned back in his chair and crossed his arms. He ignored Exeter, keeping his sharp focus on the couple in front of him. "Not many. But the general knowledge of your ladyship's abilities is not what we're here to discuss."

"So, my wife is to be the scapegoat for murder because she's foreign, is that it?"

Crouse twitched at the growl that underlaid Rob's words. Kane prepared to pull power, to defend Rob or Zhinu or even Sir Exeter, if the detective made any move for the gun under his suit jacket.

"Not because she's foreign," Crouse said, "but because something or someone ripped poor Ms. Khan's body to shreds. And not a werewolf." He tapped a finger on the picture near Zhinu's claws.

Sir Exeter closed the top of the folder as if that would hide away the knowledge it contained. "This is outrageous. We have ample proof that Lady Zhinu is in no way responsible for this heinous crime."

"I'm more than happy to check any alibi she might want to provide," Crouse said.

"Zhinu, you were home all evening," Rob said. "Tell them."

The woman froze under the intense stares of the men who surrounded her. She tugged her hand free from Rob's grip. "I'm sorry," Zhinu said.

"Sorry for what?" Rob asked. "I was out last night, but you were home. Which of the staff did you interact with?"

"Between approximately ten o'clock in the evening and two in the morning," Crouse said.

Kane and Toria had not stumbled through the rear entrance of the townhouse until after three.

"No one." Zhinu's whisper highlighted her naked fear. "I didn't talk to any of them."

"Well, you were home, were you not?" Sir Exeter asked. "I'm sure one of them can account for your presence, even if you did not speak to them."

Zhinu shook her head without a word.

"What does that mean?" Rob recaptured his wife's hand. "You weren't home?"

She shook her head again.

All the blood had rushed from Kane's face, and the entire scenario took on the aura of a farce watched from a distance. Zhinu had not played her expected role. She was supposed to deny all involvement. The police would then apologize for the mistake, promise to destroy the records showing Zhinu's other form, and let them go home. Next to him, Toria clenched her fists so hard that Kane's palms ached in sympathy.

"Lady Wallace, you must show the detective that there is no way you had anything to do with this," Sir Exeter said. "Even if you left the house unaccompanied, as is your right, there must be someone else who can verify that you were nowhere near…"

"Foundry Laboratories," Crouse said, impassive.

Kane gave the detective credit. The man betrayed no eagerness to catch Zhinu out, that he wanted to blame the foreign woman no matter what.

"Yes, precisely," said Sir Exeter. "Where were you?"

The men stared at Zhinu, who seemed to shrink in on herself with misery. "I can't. I'm sorry."

"Zhinu, please, my love." Rob pleaded as if he might drop to his knees at any moment. "Tell Detective Crouse what he needs to prove you had no involvement in this mess. We can go home, and the police can catch the real killer."

If anything, Rob's plaintiveness stiffened Zhinu's resolve. She straightened in her seat and sucked in a steadying breath.

Kane's heart fell. Rob's pleas would go unfulfilled.

"I was not at home during that time, so the household staff cannot vouch for my whereabouts," Zhinu said, her voice strengthening by the word. "And I am unable to provide an alibi for the time during which this crime was committed."

The drop of a pin would have echoed through the room like a gunshot in the silence that followed.

"Right, then." Detective Crouse collected his folder and stood. "I'll give you time to discuss options with your lawyer, Lady Wallace. But if you're unable to clear your name, I'm afraid you will remain a key suspect in this investigation." He exited the room without a backward glance.

Rob and Exeter spoke together, Rob's franticness clashing with the lawyer's lecturing tone. Between them, Zhinu huddled in on herself, staring down at the table.

They all missed Toria's whisper, meant for Kane's ears alone. "What the hell do we do now?"

Kane and Toria had dragged clients out of barroom brawls, helped them avoid the outraged spouses of illicit lovers, and on one memorable occasion, fled a country house party with nothing but the clothes on their backs.

A murder charge was new territory.

Zhinu's misery saturated the unmarked police town-car. Toria sat next to her in silence, the countryside flashing by in a blur lit by the occasional streetlamp. The time before dawn was always the darkest, but this night had already dragged on for days.

Whether in deference to Zhinu's station or because the police thought they held Toria hostage against the weredragon's good behavior, at least they had been together since Zhinu's arrest at the prince's manor. Now, Toria accompanied Zhinu to the Wallace country estate, two hours outside Londinium by car, where the noblewoman would be under house arrest for the duration of the murder investigation.

No amount of pleading by Rob, Sir Exeter, or even Toria or Kane had forced Zhinu to reveal her location or activity during the evening in question. She refused to state where she had gone or who might have accompanied her. Nothing that would allow Detective Crouse to consider Zhinu anything other than a person of interest in the case.

However, her station did mean Zhinu would not be put in general custody or even sequestered away in a cell used for uncontrollable werewolves. Whether due to Sir Exeter's manipulations or because word had come from on high, the detective agreed with Zhinu's confinement to the house and immediate gardens of the couple's country property.

Zhinu clutched her hands together as if they drove to her death, not an opulent mansion. Toria found no sympathy for her friend under the current circumstances, and the ride passed in silence.

Rob promised to send word to the estate to prepare for their arrival, and when they rolled up the long drive, lights shone across a dark lawn. Toria waited as the armed driver and his partner stopped the vehicle. Two large vans followed, and a squadron of police officers poured out before the driver opened Toria's door.

"Thank you," she said, ignoring the shock that rippled across the driver's face at her politeness. But she was not the one in trouble, and her cooperation could do more good than harm in these circumstances.

Exhaustion plucked at her as she darted around the town-car to help Zhinu out the other side. Zhinu clutched at Toria's arm to maintain her balance on the gravel drive in her heels, meant more for dancing than walking across a country road.

The front door burst open, and the estate's housekeeper hurried down the front steps. "Lady Zhinu! Oh, my poor dear." The police officers stiffened at her approach, but the older woman paid them no mind. "Let's get you inside. You're not even wearing a wrap!"

Toria had encountered the formidable woman who ran Rob's childhood home with an iron fist on previous visits. Though his parents had retired to the shore, leaving the family title and control of their financial empire in their son's capable hands, Mrs. Hamilton had declared herself too old to change her ways. Other supernatural creatures beside werewolves made their home in Britannia, and when a werebear claimed her territory, even her nominal employers did not dare to argue.

"Excuse me, ma'am." A woman with an insignia on her collar blocked the housekeeper's path. "We're here to ensure that Lady Wallace does not leave the premises."

"You do that." Mrs. Hamilton did not pause to allow further conversation as she led Zhinu past the guards. "Come along, Toria. Can't have the two of you catching your deaths in this cold."

Dew coated the surfaces around them, but the coolness of the air did not even prickle the skin on Toria's exposed arms. Mrs. Hamilton did not hesitate to use the force of her personality to sweep them inside, and the police milled about in confusion as Mrs. Hamilton's son Walter shut the door behind them.

Her expression shifted from absent-minded older woman to piercing predator the moment they were ensconced in the foyer. "Robert called about your arrival. Something about a murder accusation. Did you kill someone, Zhinu?"

Rob and Zhinu might own the house, but this was the bear's territory through and through. Zhinu bowed to the housekeeper, reverting to the ingrained manners of her Qin upbringing in her overwhelmed state. "No, Mrs. Hamilton. I swear it."

"But you'll do nothing to clear your name?"

A refrain of the same argument that had gone in circles back in the police precinct, but with new voices. Toria settled on the bench inside the front door. She had no reason to hope Zhinu might change her tune this time.

With a cluck of irritation at the ensuing silence, Mrs. Hamilton said, "Nothing to do about it now. I suppose that lot will be here for the foreseeable future." She narrowed her eyes at Toria, as if holding her personally responsible for the inconvenience.

"Yes." This information, at least, Toria could provide. "They'll set up a mobile command center in the morning—this morning. Zhinu is to stay in the house, and she's allowed on the grounds under direct police supervision." So said the deal Sir Exeter hammered out with Detective Crouse and his superiors.

"Walt, put the kettle on," Mrs. Hamilton said. "They'll need loads of tea. Zhinu, I put fresh sheets on the bed in your suite. The two of you can share tonight. Robert said he and Kane would arrive with luggage for you both in the morning." The younger werebear, bulky and silent as always, vanished toward the kitchen as his mother directed.

Zhinu bowed low again. "Thank you, Mrs. Hamilton."

"Off to bed with the both of you. We'll speak at a more civilized hour." Without waiting for a response, the housekeeper followed her son.

Toria heaved herself off the bench, but Zhinu did not move. Toria curled an arm around her shoulders. "Come on. I'm exhausted, so I know you are."

As Zhinu allowed Toria to tug her upstairs, she said, "You're not going to berate me, too?"

"What's the point?" Up the grand staircase, down the hallway to the master suite. Toria and Kane often shared a suite on the third floor, but tonight she would take the other half of the enormous bed Zhinu shared with Rob here.

Once inside, Zhinu sagged against the shut door. "Everyone else is furious with me."

Toria paused in changing out of her formal slacks and blouse into one of the nightgowns laid out on the bed. "I'm not furious. I know for a fact that neither is Kane. And I doubt Rob is."

"Rob has the most reason to be furious. Help me with my zipper?" Zhinu presented her back to Toria. "I caused enough scandal when he brought me to Britannia and broke off his previous engagement. That was nothing compared to this."

As Toria played makeshift lady's maid, she said, "I imagine Rob is more worried about you than anything else. Worried and scared." She helped Zhinu step out of her evening finery and handed her the other nightgown.

66

Without a word, Zhinu crossed into the bathroom and closed the door behind her. Water for the shower ran but did not block out the hitching sobs that reached Toria's ears.

What a mess. Toria unhooked her bra under the nightgown, tossed it over her clothes, and climbed into the giant bed. Despite the physical distance between them, she pushed love and affection through her bond with Kane. He and Rob would be here in a matter of hours, and they could figure out what to do together. Until then, she could do nothing for the sobbing weredragon who had brought all of this upon herself.

Rob did not ask Toria and Kane to keep his wife in their sight at all times at the country estate, nor did the warrior-mage pair make a formal agreement about it. It just happened. Zhinu handled the constant supervision without complaint for nearly forty-eight hours. Her patience snapped when Toria settled onto a library couch with a book, replacing Kane as soon as he vacated the spot in search of an afternoon snack.

"I am not a child," Zhinu said. She kept her attention on the letter she wrote at a desk in the corner, but the scratch of her pen across paper grew sharp.

"That is accurate." Fewer than two years separated them in age. Closer to eighteen months, but Toria had finally decided not to bother accounting for the time spent in Nacostina.

"Why do I never get a moment alone, even in my own house?"

Toria made a show of ignoring Zhinu. She turned the page of her book without reading a word. "Sheer coincidence, I assure you."

"You're being a bitch."

"Takes one to know one." Never in a million years would Toria deign to speak to any other client in such a manner, but this was Zhinu.

As expected, her friend huffed in irritation and proceeded to ignore Toria for the next hour. Morning sunlight poured through the library's tall windows, and the thermal travel mug of tea at Toria's elbow stayed warm without the use of excess magic. She could imagine no better way to spend a lazy spring day, and by the time Zhinu stood from her desk, Toria had stopped pretending to read as the thriller absorbed her interest.

Toria prepared to drag herself away from the action-filled story, but Zhinu dropped onto the opposite couch in an artless sprawl. "Cancelled all my engagements for the next few weeks. Like a polite lady should."

"That's what you get for being a polite lady."

"Not sure why I bothered. I'm sure no one wants an accused murderer at their daughter's tenth birthday party." Zhinu trailed one arm off the edge of the couch and traced the carpet pattern.

Now Toria did pull herself out of the story. She set aside the book after marking her place with a scrap of paper. "Depends on the kid. I'd have been delighted, I'm sure."

A burst of giggles escaped Zhinu, a welcome sound after dark clouds hovered over her the past two days. "Same here. Can you imagine if we'd grown up together? We'd have been hellions."

An understatement, based on how Toria's mother had often lamented the hijinks Toria and Kane managed. "But it'd have been a blast."

"Instead, I was treated like a china doll for my mother to use to gain court influence. I thank my ancestors every day that Robert stumbled into my life."

The library was private. For the first time since the arrest, Zhinu seemed open to conversation. But Toria could not flat-out ask the woman why she refused to provide an alibi and release herself from this self-imposed prison. They could go to Londinium, forget this had ever happened. Let the police patrolling the estate return to their jobs.

Whether Zhinu had murdered Sarnai Khan was not the question here. But the longer this dragged on, the more it seemed like whatever Zhinu hid was just as dangerous. Why would she put herself in this position? Why put Rob through this?

Rob. Zhinu had mentioned him herself. Toria would thread this conversation with care. "I feel the same about Kane and I finding each other."

Zhinu stared past Toria, out the window behind her. "If not for Robert, I'd still be trapped in that palace, married to my cousin. I adored Yu, but he was like an elder brother to me. I'd be obliged to do my best to provide an heir, but the idea of it—" Her shudder expressed her disgust with more elegance than words ever could.

Toria could imagine all too well. And if Zhinu could share, so could she. "Sounds familiar. People kept trying to force Kane and me into a relationship when we were teenagers."

"But, he does not…"

"Nope." The idea of Kane with a woman in any sort of sexual situation was laughable, and Toria had the embarrassing first-hand experience to prove it.

"But he found his Archer. And am I to understand that your newfound status will break plenty of hearts back in Oxenafor?"

One of the many perks of acting as Zhinu's bodyguard during her time at university included the surplus of handsome young men with plenty of interest in an exotic foreign woman and an equal lack of interest in conversation the morning after. Romance had nothing to do with it. Until an elf with expressive eyes and intellectual curiosity to match her own swept her off her feet in a doomed city. "I think Liam is planning to stick around." He did wait decades for the chance, after all.

The pleasure that bloomed on Zhinu's face almost made Toria forget her companion's awkward position. Almost.

"That makes me so happy for you," Zhinu said. "Perhaps I will get to meet him someday. Tell me about him"

Toria ignored the imperiousness of the order. If Zhinu wanted girl talk, Toria was happy to talk up her relationship with Liam. Make Zhinu think about her relationship with Rob and how this situation might be affecting him.

Not that talking about Liam was a terrible hardship, even leaving out the full story of how they met. The fewer people who learned about time travel, the better. So, Liam and Toria met when he returned to teach at the university in Limani. Simple as that.

"You know I'm not romantic. That's Kane's department. But there was something about him."

"Well, you know romance had nothing to do with my relationship with Robert."

According to Toria's mother, who witnessed the contract between Rob and Zhinu after Zhinu proposed to her werewolf lord, the innocent bystanders had been more irritated at the entire situation than awestruck. "But you two have made it work."

"It has been work," Zhinu said. "But he made the time to court me during my studies, while he trained to take over for his parents. All I wanted was an education and a new life as my own woman. I never thought I'd be fodder for tabloids and attending parties with royalty."

Good girl, Zhinu. A bit more prodding, and Toria would have her right where she wanted her. "All I wanted was a life in my mom's footsteps. My family and steady work. No more entanglements than I already had." As much as she enjoyed tutoring students on a casual basis at the mage school in Limani, she had always been ready to leave again. Until she visited the past and came home to find Liam waiting for her.

"And then, Liam happened?" Almost like Zhinu could read her mind.

"That he did."

"And he's a professor, right? What does he think about you leaving home?"

Now the conversation echoed Kane's line of questioning from the bar. "We kind of didn't talk about it."

But unlike Kane's burst of shock, Zhinu said, "I understand. Robert and I never really talked about it either. We have such different lives and goals, but we work together. Differences that complement each other. I hope you and Liam can manage that, too."

Toria forced her posture to remain relaxed. She breathed deep to keep her heart rate steady so that Zhinu's heightened hearing would not notice how much stress this conversation caused. She had intended to remind Zhinu that her relationship with Rob was the most important thing, except Zhinu already knew that in her soul.

Toria's relationship anxiety was not the purpose of this discussion, but she had no clear plan on how to fix this topic derailment. "I hope so, too." And for a moment, she allowed herself to ache for home. Sure, she missed her family. Her bed. Even the damned students. But those were passing thoughts, in the vein of

I wish I could talk to Mom about this, or *I hope Mohinder finally learned how to stop creating power surges every time he crosses a carpet.*

Now, she wanted nothing more than to be in bed with Liam. Not even naked with him, though she would not complain about that either. But spending a quiet morning reading with him, instead of trapped in a mansion with a stubborn weredragon.

"I know you'll work it out," Zhinu said, straightening on the couch and swinging her legs to the floor. "Love is when people can walk in opposite directions and remain side by side. Come on, Mrs. Hamilton should have lunch ready soon."

Without waiting for a response, Zhinu whisked out of the library, and Toria made no effort to chase after her and keep the woman in sight. Her attempt to manipulate Zhinu into seeing the ridiculousness of the situation she had maneuvered them into had backfired. Now Toria ached with loneliness on the other side of the world from the one person she wanted to be next to.

"You've been quiet all day."

When Kane broke the silence, Toria jerked so hard she almost fell out of her armchair. "Don't scare a girl like that."

"Like you didn't know I was here." Kane dropped into the opposite armchair and stretched his long legs before him, so one bare foot brushed Toria's.

True. Even in the depths of Toria's distraction, as she stared into the empty fireplace, she always sensed when someone entered a room. "I was thinking."

"That much is obvious. Missing Liam?"

Toria ignored Kane's amusement and the poke of his foot that accompanied the tease. But she found no point in hiding where her mind had been all afternoon since her emotions leaked through their bond like a sieve. At least he couldn't complain about inappropriate daydreams when most of her circuitous musings had involved attempts to reconcile her current profession with nurturing a relationship. She was not Kane, with such a secure connection with Archer that they might as well have been the bonded pair.

"Something like that." But she had no desire to rehash the conversation with Zhinu earlier in the day, the one that had seen her silent through lunch and dinner. Time to change Kane's focus. "I'm not comfortable sitting around and waiting for Zhinu to either provide an alibi or for the police to arrest her for real, no matter what evidence they find."

"You think that might happen?"

"You think they're going to work hard to find an alternative murderer? I trust Detective Crouse when he says a werewolf didn't kill the woman. Who else in this country has claws like that?" She had glimpsed the forensic photos when armed officers escorted her and Zhinu from the interview room to a holding cell to await the ride to the country estate. Sure, Britannia had werebears and the occasional large cat. But even the largest of those did not have talons the length of dinner knives.

"What's your idea, then?"

That's what she loved about Kane. One of the many things, at least. Despite her anxiety issues, he did not dismiss her fears out of hand. And he trusted her to have a plan in place already to deal with them.

"Regardless of what our contract says," Toria said. "This isn't a traditional bodyguard gig anymore."

Kane laughed. "It never was. That's what we get for being friends with the clients."

Toria flicked her fingers. "Aside from that. I'm not talking about smuggling her out of the country before she gets arrested. Rob would never stand for that."

"More like Rob's team of lawyers wouldn't stand for that. Frankly, Exeter terrifies me."

"No, we have to clear her name."

Instead of leaping to immediate agreement or dismissal of the idea, Kane stroked the evening stubble that coated his chin. "That is not in our contract."

"But as you said, she's a friend."

"Sitting around here is a waste of our extensive skill sets."

Delight surged through Toria, which Kane matched and returned. But reality tempered her next words. "We're not trained investigators, though, despite those extensive skill sets."

"We shouldn't recreate whatever the police are doing anyway," Kane said. "They don't need two bumbling amateur detectives impeding their work."

"But the police aren't professional followers, which you are. I think you should go with Rob when he returns to Londinium tomorrow." After all, the Wallace empire continued to march on, regardless of what scandal embroiled the family.

"Right," Kane said. "Because this might not be about Zhinu. She could be a scapegoat for some sort of plot against Rob. He may have hired us to be with Zhinu, but he needs backup if he's a target, too. You'll stay here with Zhinu?"

"Not exactly."

"Tor—"

"Hear me out," she said. "We might not be investigators, but one of us has to get to that lab and check things out. And I'm in a better position to know what I'm looking at." She did not mention her lesser chance at being marked as an outsider at the busy complex due to her skin tone.

Some impressions leaked through their connection, and Kane asked, "That your polite way of telling me I stand out in a crowd?"

"Something like that. Am I wrong?"

"No," Kane said. "You'd be better at talking your way out of a situation based on whatever is in the room. And you won't panic if one of those things is a damned missile."

"Sounds like a plan."

"At least I get a trip to Londinium out of it, even if it's to follow Rob around and act menacing."

"There's nothing you do better."

Kane pulled the decorative throw pillow on the chair from behind his back and hurled it at Toria.

Kane reminded himself for the fifth or sixth time that hour alone that he had experienced more boring contracts. He drummed his fingers against his thigh and shifted his hips in another failed attempt to make the lobby chair comfortable. Comfort was not the seat's intended purpose. The black and white décor and blocky furniture meant to intimidate rather than welcome visitors.

People did not wait for Robert Wallace. They made an appointment through his secretary and arrived at the designated time.

Underneath Rob's light-hearted exterior lay a quick mind, and he followed the logic of Kane accompanying him into the city at once. Giving Toria credentials to return to Foundry Laboratories on her own had not been as easy, but he also caved on that account.

Mrs. Hamilton and her son ensured Zhinu's safety at the country estate. No one crossed a werebear family on their territory and lived to tell the tale. At this point, the police were superfluous, but their presence supported an important political point. It turned out that Sarnai Khan was a member of a protected minority class within the British Empire. This refugee community had fled the encroaching eastern Roman advancement almost fifty years ago. The Chingis community received protection from the government due to mandates laid under Queen Moira's grandfather, even though popular opinion had never sided with them.

Kane believed that people should live however they wished, as long as they hurt no one else or enforced their way of living onto others. However, part of his brain niggled over the oddness of a culture that worshiped a deity, a single deity at that, and imposed so many regulations on their community members.

Well, he would stay in his lane if they stayed in theirs. With Zhinu as the top suspect, nothing pointing to a hate crime had shown up in the investigation into Ms. Khan's death so far.

The conference room door opened, and staff members emerged. The end of the meeting cued Kane to rise from the atrocious chair and stand until Rob appeared. He chatted in the doorway with a subordinate, a quick follow-up to some point made in the meeting. Kane lurked in the hall and ignored the curious stares of those who passed by.

Once Rob concluded his conversation, Kane fell into step behind him. Now that he was on the move, his stomach provided an audible warning that breakfast had been a long drive into the city and three meetings ago. But today, he lived according to Rob's schedule.

Except not much escaped Rob's heightened senses, including stomach complaints. "Yes, I agree," he said, offhand. In the elevator, Rob selected the button for the lobby. "What sounds good for lunch?"

Since the elevator provided a moment of privacy, Kane broke professionalism and rolled his eyes. "That's not how this works."

"But you're not my bodyguard, are you? All this is for show, so I can accommodate your lunch tastes or drag you to my favorite deli near this office. They have a fantastic corned beef."

"That sounds great."

"You're not just saying that because you'd rather not express your own opinion."

"No," Kane said. "I like corned beef." Since his arrival in Britannia, he'd had no chance for it, and it was not a common find in Limani.

"Perfect."

Outside the elevator, Kane fell into step behind Rob, acting the role of professional security. It was not fashionable for a werewolf of Rob's youth to employ a bodyguard, but no one would comment on it under the circumstances. It also was not fashionable for a werewolf of Rob's station to frequent a restaurant without table service. Once Kane bit into his corned beef, he understood this particular dismissal of convention.

They found free seats at a rickety table with a street view through the plate glass window. The first time Kane spotted the man, he figured it for coincidence. He was unsure which caught his attention first: the memorable sleeves of tattoos on each arm or the glint of sunlight reflecting in the gloss of his black hair. The pickpocket from the other evening, though in a different part of the city today.

The second time, perhaps the man had taken a wrong turn.

But by the third time, it was apparent he was up to something. Considering his sleight-of-hand on their first encounter him, Kane had to assume the pickpocket was here to cause some sort of trouble.

"Back to the grind, alas," Rob said, balling the remnants of his sandwich wrapper in his hands. "I've got a one-on-one at the office. After that, we're off to tea with leaders of the shipping union. Which will be more whinging and moaning about taxes than having tea, so I'm glad we ate now."

"You go on." Kane wanted to ensure the pickpocket did not follow Rob when he left the shop.

"What happened to the act as my permanent shadow?"

"I trust you can make it three blocks on your own. There's something I want to check out."

Rob didn't question him, flicking a casual salute before exiting the shop and strolling toward his office building. Kane dangled him as potential bait, but Rob either didn't realize or didn't mind.

And there the tattooed man followed, in the same direction as Rob and at a steady distance behind. Kane slipped out of the shop behind his target. His purpose would be much easier in a more rural setting, or even an area of the city that made half an effort to include greenery amidst the concrete and stone. Instead of casting a "don't notice me" charm, Kane had to do this the old-fashioned way. Not easy when both of them stood out amidst the sea of pale British faces moving about town on a gorgeous spring afternoon.

But the tattooed man was so intent on Rob that he remained oblivious to acquiring his own shadow. When he peeled away after Rob entered the office building, Kane ducked down a narrow side street.

When the man turned a corner, Kane leaned against the wall, waiting for him.

The tattooed man paused but did not appear shocked. "I was wondering where you'd gone off to."

Kane didn't make a move for him, nor did he acknowledge the man's statement. "Why are you tracking Robert Wallace?"

The tattoos' sharp black ink stood out against the man's dark skin in the afternoon sunlight. They formed a mixture of symbols and designs, but no language or script in which Kane held knowledge.

This close, Kane's magical shields brushed against the aura of power the man emitted. But it was no elemental magic he recognized, nor did it contain traces of primal energy. Almost artificial compared to the power that Kane lived and breathed.

Giving in to the temptation to learn more, Kane pulled magesight across his vision.

The man waited with statuesque patience, and passersby flowed around them like a stream parted by two rocks. But the man before him did not wear shields similar to any Kane had ever seen before. Instead of a swirl of color, like Toria's electric prisms or his own sheltering canopy of thick leaves, the man's sported hues of muted grays and blues, and crawling lines of power seemed to connect to certain of his tattoos. As if the ink itself provided his protective barrier.

Kane recoiled, dropping his magesight until a plain man stood before him once more. His single experience with magical tattoos had not been a good one. He lashed out, pinning the man in place against the wall with a grip on his thick shoulder. "What's your business with Earl Wallace? Who the hell are you?"

The man glanced at Kane's hand but made no move to escape. "I am Gan Baatar. Sarnai Khan was my cousin."

"If you seek vengeance," Kane said, "the Wallaces had nothing to do with her death."

"I know." Gan dropped his shoulder out of Kane's hand and stepped aside. "But Sarnai's father, who banished her from the family over ten years ago, now seeks redemption for his selfishness."

Kane did not care about their family politics. "Either way, you're after the wrong guy." His fingers tingled where they had touched Gan, but he resisted the urge to wipe them on his pants to dull the effect.

Gan stepped away as if testing whether Kane would come after him. When Kane did not move, Gan made a show of dragging his attention over Kane's body. "My cousin was an only child. I am the third son."

Kane stilled under Gan's study. "What's that supposed to mean?"

"That perhaps I am after the wrong guy." At that, Gan melted into a cluster of passing businessmen.

He should not have managed to disappear in a group of suits while dressed in battered jeans and another too-tight shirt. But magic swept the sidewalk, and Kane lost him again.

The credentials Rob gave her allowed Toria unimpeded and unescorted access to all parts of Foundry Laboratories. But he had warned her that morning, when he handed over the letter, that she needed to come up with a reason for being there other than intellectual curiosity.

As Dr. Tierney tapped her foot in the central security vestibule, Toria considered that she should have given Rob's words more credence. Her attempt at charming did nothing to soften Dr. Tierney's glare.

The best lies always contained an element of truth. "I'm sure you've heard the news," Toria said, "of Lady Wallace's house arrest. Since my services are not currently needed, her husband has allowed me to pursue one of my side passions rather than have me rattle about their country estate."

"And what side passion might that be?"

Sarcasm dripped from Tierney's words, and Toria could not blame her. She did not come off as the intellectual sort, not with a rapier at her hip and build of a woman who lived by her strength. But as her mother would say, Toria contained hidden depths, and she was not afraid to use them. "Before my partner and I left Limani, we realized that radio frequencies once again allowed for long-distance communication without the benefit of elven assistance. I was looking forward to discussing my discoveries with anyone on your staff doing the same sort of research."

"I fail to see how you could contribute anything to the conversation."

Toria never let her attitude of open friendliness slip as she adjusted the satchel that hung off her shoulder. "I believe the earl hoped that if he was to pay me for a contract I'm unable to fulfill, I should instead make myself useful in other ways that might benefit his family."

Dr. Tierney pursed her lips, her distaste for the suggestion evident in how her skin paled under her lip gloss. "I suppose you can wait in a secure room while I see whether Dr. Reese has a moment to speak to you."

She turned on her heel, and Toria followed her through a maze of hallways and covered walkways until they arrived at a generic office. Despite Rob's orders, Dr. Tierney did not seem keen on allowing Toria free run of the lab.

"I can't guarantee that Dr. Reese will be free anytime soon," Dr. Tierney said once Toria had settled herself in a seat in front of the empty desk.

The vacant office was bare of personality, and the astringent smell of cleaning chemicals tickled Toria's nose. "I'm more than happy to wait," she said. Toria retrieved a notepad from her satchel and flicked through the pages. "I have lots to chat with Dr. Reese about, and it's better than babysitting."

Her gamble paid off. The muscles in Dr. Tierney's face unfroze enough for her glare to soften. "Yes, I felt similar when you visited the lab a few days ago." The researcher might understand who paid her bills, but she didn't have to like the hoops she jumped through to keep the lights on.

"Go on," Toria said. "I don't want to keep you any longer. I'll be here when your colleague has time for me."

Dr. Tierney did not deign to thank Toria for her consideration, but she left the office with a final admonishment for Toria to stay put.

Well, to hell with that. Once Dr. Tierney's footsteps faded, Toria stood. She pulled magesight across her vision and blinked into the added brightness under the windowless office's fluorescent lights. Dull beiges and grays. A vacant office, with no permanent occupant to imprint their sense of self on the space, either physically or magically.

Toria peered out the open doorway. The chemical aroma was more pungent out here, but she hadn't noticed when distracted by Dr. Tierney. Now, she followed her nose down the hallway to an office a few doors down.

The door stood ajar a mere inch, but this was the source of the sharp tang in the air. When Toria swung open the door all the way, she flinched. Not from the smell but from the aura of terror that saturated the space.

Such things as ghosts did not exist, but certain people with enough sensitivity could sense echoes of events that permeated a location. Any strong emotion did the trick, but panic and rage tended to stick around the longest.

No visual evidence remained in this office of a woman's murder. But even with the scene of the crime scrubbed clean following any necessary police work, Toria's magesight all but screamed that this was where Sarnai Khan died.

She breathed through her mouth, both to clear her sinuses of the heavy scent of bleach and to calm her roiling stomach. Even though none of the gore in the crime scene photographs remained, the echoes of Sarnai's screams rasped against her psyche like nails on a chalkboard.

Beyond the putrid aura of terror, Toria's magesight picked out slivers of pastel pink and sparkling gold that remained in the space. The echoes of Sarnai's life, along with her death. This office had been hers. Toria forced herself a step farther into the room. Then another. She braced both hands on the empty desk and dove into the room's essence.

Like swimming through sludge, with pockets of freshwater that clung to Toria's skin once they found her. Sarnai must have had a touch of magic, though Toria had missed it during their brief encounter. Now, the leftover bits of Sarnai's power sought out the equivalent of sympathetic magic, desperate to escape the dark stain of her death.

And if touches of her power remained here, it meant the remnants of a set-spell Sarnai had cast somewhere in the room. Without Sarnai to feed the charm strength, the spell would fail on its own. Before that, Toria could use its trace to find it.

She opened her physical eyes again, not sure when she had closed them. Swirls of fear and pain still saturated the room, but a faint glow at a corner ceiling tile caught her attention. It was identical to the rest except for that tingle of power. It screamed its presence to those with the ability to sense it.

Toria shoved a nearby credenza under the corner and stepped onto it. She brushed the ceiling tile with the tips of her fingers. No physical reaction, no shock or burn. Not a protective spell, at least. She nudged the ceiling tile up and to the side, then reached inside.

Nothing except dust. A speck drifted into Toria's eye, and she wiped it away, tears filling her vision. Her magesight dropped, and she stood in an empty office, with no hint that anything tragic had ever occurred here except for the itch at the back of her neck.

She needed to return to where Tierney had instructed her to wait before Dr. Reese, or worse, Tierney herself, found her poking around. She replaced the credenza in its original position.

But she also needed to visit this office later, when she had enough time to search for whatever Sarnai had left.

Rob stayed the night in Londinium because of an early appointment the next morning, but he sent Kane to the country estate. However, when Kane returned to the large house in time for a late dinner, he dined with Zhinu alone.

"I've had no word from her since she left," Zhinu said, pushing food around her plate. They shared a meal in the casual back parlor instead of eating as a pair in the cavernous dining room. "You've sensed nothing?"

"No, I can't." The film Kane picked to accompany them played on the television, volume low. Neither was in the mood for a romantic comedy, even a new release. "Distance becomes a factor. I can tell she's alive, obviously, but anything more at this range would have to be an incredibly strong sending."

Zhinu exchanged her half-empty plate for her wine glass. She pulled her legs onto the couch and tucked herself under a lap blanket. Despite the tapestries that warmed the walls in this cozy room, the older section of the mansion retained a chill.

"It must be lovely," Zhinu said, running a finger around the rim of her glass, "to never be alone."

Kane didn't have the heart to insist on any sort of propriety after that comment, but he could not help the snort of laugher that escaped around his mouthful of food. Once he managed to swallow without choking, Kane said, "Toria and I have been bonded for over half our lives now. I would have given anything for a moment's peace plenty of times those first few years."

"She told me about Liam the other day." For a woman who complained that the other British nobility did nothing but gossip, Zhinu seemed keen on digging for it at the moment. "I'm so happy that's working out."

Kane assumed this was where he was supposed to give his opinion of the man, but he found it hard to separate his personal thoughts from Toria's obvious adoration. There was also the added wrinkle that, in a way, Kane owed his existence to Liam since the elven man had rescued Kane's great-great-grandfather from a doomed city. "Liam is a good man," Kane said. The absolute truth, at least.

"Handsome?"

"Very."

"I would expect nothing less."

They shared a moment of laughter, and Kane snatched the television remote to resume the movie. But a tap at the door interrupted them, and Mrs. Hamilton entered.

"Zhinu, a man is here to visit you." Worry lines creased Mrs. Hamilton's face. "The police searched him and permitted him to enter the house. I stuck him in the library, but it would make me feel better if Kane chaperoned."

"Since when do I need a chaperone?" Zhinu asked.

"Since the gentlemen said his name was Gan Baatar, and that he's a relative of the poor woman who died," Mrs. Hamilton said, her voice tart. "I won't have anything happening to him and the blame pinned on you."

"That makes perfect sense," Kane said before Zhinu could argue further. He also wanted to learn what the man following Rob earlier that day wanted with Zhinu, and that meant he wasn't about to leave her alone with him either. He set aside the remote and his plate.

They rose from the couch as one, but Zhinu ran her hands down the plain tunic she wore with leggings. "Kane, please entertain our guest while I change into something more appropriate."

Zhinu disappeared up the rear staircase while Kane proceeded through the house. He still wore the business attire, trousers and button-up shirt, he used to fade into Rob's background that day, though divested of the concealed weapons once ensconced in the country estate's nominal safety. Now, Kane strengthened his shields as he drew his fingers along wooden and stone walls to pull energy from the old building itself. If Gan proved to be a threat, he could extend his shielding to Zhinu long enough to call for assistance.

Knowing the formidable Mrs. Hamilton, she had already asked her son to change shape and lurk nearby, and she needed the barest excuse to transform and come to the rescue as well.

When Kane slipped into the library, Gan turned away from the bookshelf he perused. He had put some effort into dressing for the meeting—a long-sleeved button-up that strained across the shoulders rather than the comfortably worn-in T-shirts Kane had seen on their previous encounters. His long hair draped over his shoulder in a thick braid.

Kane spared a moment to regret a missed glimpse of the man's fascinating tattoos and said, "Good evening. Lady Wallace will join us shortly."

"Good evening." After returning the greeting, Gan drifted along the shelves until he paused before a set of old law books. "Interesting collection."

"Those probably belonged to the earl's father or grandfather," Kane said. He leaned one hip against a couch. "The current holder of the title attended business school instead."

"How lucky for the Wallaces to have the space to keep around outdated texts." Gan's finger traced the spine of a book, where the title had worn away with age. "I grew up in a room shared with two cousins and my brother."

Gan's discomfort with the surrounding opulence expressed itself in how he avoided the plush rugs that broke up the desk and sitting areas. He completed a circle of the room until he faced Kane.

Kane hesitated to question Gan's presence without Zhinu, so a staring match ensued. Gan's gaze was like a physical touch against Kane's skin, but the previous note of sexual attraction had vanished. Instead, they sized each other up like predators, and Kane drew another dose of power from the earth below the house. Gan's mouth quirked as if he understood what Kane had done. But before he could comment, the library door burst open.

Zhinu strode in with the click of heels, skirt fluttering around her knees like an encroaching wave. When she came to a halt, the three stood as if on points of a triangle. "I am Lady Zhinu Wallace. You wished to see me?"

Gan offered her a sort of bow. "I appreciate your time, Lady Wallace. I am called Gan Baatar. I wished to speak to you regarding your involvement with my people in Londinium."

As in the news reports about his cousin's identity, Gan must be referring to the small group of Chingis that lived within Britannia. But where Kane expected Zhinu to deny any knowledge, she instead slid a hesitant glance in Kane's direction and said, "And what about it? I never met Ms. Khan before I encountered her at Foundry Laboratories."

"My cousin's father is adamant that you be punished for her murder."

Zhinu tapped one finger against her chin. "Khan…. Is your cousin's father that stubborn man who insists I wear gloves when I share tea with his family as if my nails will contaminate the biscuits? I never even knew he had a daughter."

"Cousin Tomor had a falling out with his daughter when she wished to pursue an education over accepting the marriage he arranged for her," Gan said.

A muscle at his temple jumped as if that explanation hit closer to home than he wished to let on.

Zhinu scoffed. "And British law supersedes certain of your people's religious customs."

"Wait," Kane said, unable to hold it in any longer. "How do you know all of this? How do you know the dead woman's father? You've had tea with him?"

"Not with him, of course," Zhinu said. "Honestly, I shouldn't even be allowed in the same room as our guest here without my husband or female chaperone because he is an unmarried man." Gan nodded at her assumption. "The first thing I did once I settled in this country was search for a taste of the familiar. The small Chingis community in Oxenafor embraced me, but I have found that sense of inclusion more difficult since I moved to Londinium and married Robert."

"Because those who live in Oxenafor are more relaxed in their traditions," Gan said. "Whereas in Londinium, many of the families seem to do their best to live as if they never left the steppes of lower Rus."

That explained a lot. Once Rob had spirited her out of the Qin colonies, Zhinu had become a woman without a country. "But what does this have to do with your accusation of Sarnai Khan's murder?"

Zhinu pursed her lips. "As I said, in Oxenafor, I was just another student. And I've never been a true part of the Chingis community. We share the barest hints of heritage, a few words of vocabulary, some familiar cooking techniques. Now, I belong to the social elite."

Gan unbuttoned his cuffs and rolled up his shirt sleeves as if unable to handle the confining fabric any longer. "I was escorting my mother to services and overheard the elders debating whether to let you meet the women."

"Because I'm such a terrible influence, I'm sure."

"I am not an elder," Gan said, shrugging one shoulder.

The conversation bounced between them with tennis-like intensity, and Kane called a time-out. "Zhinu, does Rob know you're still involved with this community?"

She dropped her gaze and tucked a lock of loose hair behind her ear.

Kane made a mental note never to let her gamble at cards, but he had already figured out the direction this conversation pointed like a neon sign. "And that's where you were the night of the murder," he said, rubbing a hand on his face. "Why you won't alibi yourself."

Zhinu spread her hands, helpless. "It would cause so many problems for Robert if it were known that Earl Wallace's wife socialized with the Chingis."

"And that's why I'm here," Gan said. "Because that's the least of your problems now."

Kane stepped to the side as if to block Zhinu from an invisible attack. "What does that mean?"

"Tomor Khan would be more than happy to tell the world where you were the night his precious daughter died," Gan said, sarcasm obvious, "if it means the police stop paying attention to you and catch the real killer instead."

"Oh, hell." Zhinu stepped around the couch and collapsed onto it, burying her face in her hands. "What a mess."

Kane glared at Gan for lack of anywhere else to target his anger. "Why are you here?" Numerous options offered themselves, from blackmail to other forms of extortion. If Gan and Zhinu didn't even know each other due to the community's strict gender divide, what did he get out of warning her?

"Call it a 'fuck you' to my uncle," Gan said, malice sharpening his expression. "Sarnai didn't deserve what her father did to her. And I won't let Tomor ruin another woman for the sake of his pride."

Zhinu wiped away tears. "I don't deserve your kindness, Mr. Baatar."

"Yeah, well, there's not much else I can do." Gan shoved his hands in his pockets. "Your husband seems like a nice enough bloke, for a nobleman, and I've never been keen on how the elders think they can take advantage of the freedoms of this country when it suits them. Though from the stories I've heard, it's a damned sight better than when we were in Rus." He paused as if remembering to whom he spoke. "Your pardon, ma'am."

Zhinu tilted her head and examined Gan. If she had been a mage, an echo of magesight in her eyes would not have surprised Kane. "You were the one Sarnai was supposed to marry, weren't you?"

Gan shrugged one shoulder again. Not a refutation to her statement.

"Huh," Kane said. Even aside from what he'd figured out of Gan's preferences, a marriage contract made before Khan threw out his daughter meant the two must have been young teens. No wonder Sarnai ran.

"Trust me," Zhinu said. "I am no stranger to the lengths people will go to make what they think is a perfect marriage match, regardless of the opinions of the two people to be married. I assume you'd prefer your presence here did not spread beyond the estate."

"I gave the police a fake name," Gan said. "My older brother. The good son in the family came to pay his respects to the falsely accused lady of the house."

Whereas Kane's tattooed pickpocket sported a criminal record, such that visiting Zhinu would raise too many questions.

"Thank you, Mr. Baatar." Zhinu stood and bowed, which he returned. "Is there anything else you need?"

"I walked from the station," Gan said, referencing the nearest mill town. "And train fare back to Londinium wouldn't be amiss."

Zhinu crossed the library to a desk and rifled through a drawer until she emerged with a bit of cash. She handed it to Kane instead of Gan. "Please show our visitor out, Kane." Despite her tear-stained cheeks, Lady Wallace was back in place.

"Right this way." Without argument, Gan followed Kane from the room.

Darkness had fallen, and Kane recognized a city boy. Instead of letting Gan traipse the miles to town, requiring time that would put him after the final train to Londinium left even if he made no wrong turns along the way, Kane directed him to the town-car on loan from Rob.

Gan whistled through his teeth when he settled in the front passenger seat. "Not sure I've ever been in a ride this swank. This how all the top-percent live?"

"Most, yeah," Kane said. A handful of Britannia's noble families had lost their fortunes over the centuries but retained their rank based on their fellow werewolves' sufferance. Not like the vampires of the Roman Empire, who traced a direct blood lineage thousands of years and had the savings accounts to prove it.

Despite the distraction of Gan's arrival, Kane did not miss how Toria had yet to return to the country estate. Anxiety rippled under his skin, and he clutched the steering wheel with both hands.

At least Kane had a source of distraction at hand. Gan scratched one elbow in the hollow silence of the drive, seemingly unsure where to put his hands. The tattoos on his bare forearms faded into the darkness as they drove through pitch-black farmland.

"Nice ink, by the way," Kane said. He had been in no position to learn from the tattooed Roman mage he'd encountered so many years ago, but now he had a captive audience to interrogate. Politely, of course.

Gan's attention flicked from the road to Kane's hands on the steering wheel. "Same, man. Elven?"

With his arms outstretched to drive, Kane's shirt sleeves had pulled away enough to reveal the band of looping elven runes that encircled his right wrist. "Good eye."

"Not sure I've ever seen elven language tattoos on a human," Gan said. "It have something to do with you being a mage?"

Perhaps the interrogation ran both ways, but Kane did not mind Gan's curiosity. "Nah, they're the names of good friends." *Torialanthas Connor. Syrisinia. Archer Sophin.*

"Lucky man to have such good friends."

Kane's cheeks warmed at the insinuation in Gan's words, despite how wrong he was. Kane hadn't intended the conversation to go in this direction. Time to redirect. "I've got one other, on my shoulder blade." His scimitar crossed with Toria's rapier, twin to the design beneath the nape of Toria's neck. "Not sure I have the patience to sit for full sleeves."

Gan moved his arms as if to examine them in the dim light. "Started small, but never stopped, I guess. Didn't do it all at once."

"It's a bunch of smaller images?"

"Pretty much, yeah. Where I had the room."

"Any significance, or you liked the designs?"

Gan did not answer immediately. "I'm not an idiot, Nalamas. I know mages can sense energy. Ask what you want to know, yeah?" He tugged at his sleeves, despite the warmth in the car.

"They're magic." Kane didn't bother phrasing it as a question.

"Not all, but some."

The mage who had been part of the Roman forces during the invasion of Limani, before Kane even began the journeyman years of his mercenary career, shared little resemblance with Gan. "Part of Chingis culture? Or for another reason?"

"It's… complicated."

Kane allowed Gan his hesitation. The man had risked arrest or worse to warn Zhinu about the threat against her from his community. The last thing Kane wanted was to piss him off or make him regret that decision. He pulled the town-car to a stop outside the train station, bringing the conversation to a natural close before he could put his foot in his mouth. Instead, he put the vehicle in park.

Gan reached for the door handle. "Thanks for the ride."

Before he could open the door, Kane reached for Gan's shoulder. "Thank you for coming out here to warn Lady Wallace. I won't presume to offer anything on her behalf, but I count her as a friend. I owe you one."

Gan dipped his chin but did not respond. As a magic user himself, however untraditional, he understood the weight of that statement. He exited the vehicle with a slam of the door and loped across the empty parking lot to the station kiosk to purchase a ticket to Londinium.

Kane lifted his foot, about to return the vehicle to drive, when pain and shock and fury vibrated through his core. His skull hit the headrest as his spine arched, and he smacked the steering wheel with an open palm.

Toria.

He slammed shields, physical and mental, around himself until the connection dimmed enough for him to manage clear thought.

Wherever his partner was, whatever she was up to, she was in danger.

Protocol dictated that mercenaries should not nap while on missions, but it was a gorgeous spring afternoon, the soft grasses cushioned Toria's body, and she had hours to kill.

When Dr. Reese found Toria in the original office, waiting as promised, the two spent a pleasant hour talking shop. The radio specialist was Dr. Tierney's polar opposite, and for a moment, Toria had almost forgotten her reasons for returning to the lab.

That did not stop her from charging the magnetic lock on the building's fire door so that the mechanism failed to engage when they returned inside after chatting through Dr. Reese's smoke break.

Once she left the lab grounds on the motorcycle borrowed from the Wallace estate, it had required the effort of an afternoon stroll to park the bike behind a clutch of bushes about a mile away. There, she waited out the afternoon and evening for darkness to fall.

Her original plan included none of this. She spared a moment of guilt for her partner's worry when she did not return to the estate by dinner, and resolved to ignore the insistent emptiness of her stomach at the thought of food. Right now, her target was whatever Sarnai had hidden in her office.

The combination of darkness and a "don't see me" charm aided Toria's approach to the guard building at the property entrance. She slipped onto the property and followed the edge of the fence line. Magesight worked better than military-grade night goggles this close to the new moon. True invisibility was beyond the realm of possibility outside the ancient tales of sorcerers from centuries past, so Toria stayed out of range of the security cameras that dotted building corners while circling behind the administrative building where she met Dr. Reese that afternoon.

She picked out the bundle of electricity that marked the security camera above the door she had jiggered and zapped it with a power surge. Crossing mental fingers, she sprinted across the open ground to the rear door. She grasped the handle and pulled—it swung open on oiled hinges without a sound.

By the time the security camera returned online, no one would be the wiser regarding her entrance.

Toria squinted in the dim hallway, back braced against the door. Her fingers flexed, and she touched the rapier at her waist like a lucky charm.

One fluorescent light in every four cast light on the tiled floor. No light shone from any of the offices along the corridor, so anyone working late must be in their lab space. Toria crept through the hallway, counting doors until she reached Sarnai's office.

Not that it would be hard to miss. With magesight active, the emotional echoes roiled—an oily stain in the air itself. Toria forced down psychosomatic nausea.

"It's okay, Sarnai," Toria said, muttering under her breath and ignoring the absurdity of reassuring the remnant aura of a dead woman. She pushed open the office door. Nothing had changed since earlier in the afternoon. "Let's see what you've got for me."

Toria clambered atop the credenza again to push the ceiling tile out of the way. She shoved her hands, fingers spread wide, into the open space above her. Since her physical sight was useless in the darkness, she closed her eyes. The gold and pastel marking Sarnai's power had faded more in the intervening time, but enough of it lingered for Toria to thread her energy into its midst.

Sarnai's residual energy flared where it met Toria's. But whatever magical power the woman had possessed paled in comparison to Toria's ability. Toria squeezed her eyes shut tighter as if that would help her identify the set-spell. The shields Sarnai had placed around this corner of the office shattered.

When Toria re-opened her eyes, the sickening sensation of Sarnai's death had eased, as if she had appeased whatever forced a bit of Sarnai to linger in this space. But the golden glow remained. She patted around in the ceiling grid's opening until her fingers brushed a hard edge. Straining on tip-toes, Toria extended her arm far enough to grab the object.

She withdrew a spiral-bound notebook. Plain green cover. Nothing special about it. She used them herself to jot notes about various projects at home.

But when Toria flipped through the pages, it was apparent that the language within was nothing she recognized, even in the darkness. Most of the characters were Loquella, but she identified a few as the runic language used by the original inhabitants of Britannia's isles and even a few letters in flowing elven.

A code.

"Guess you couldn't make it easy for me, hon." The puke-colored clouds cleared further. The notebook was necessary, then. Toria shoved it in her satchel and fixed the ceiling tile back in place.

A door slammed in the distance. Toria froze. Footsteps? No, a different sort of gait. The squeak of rubber on tile, with too many limbs for one person. She crouched on the credenza, hidden in the shadows and protected from anyone who might pass by.

But the footsteps did not sound humanoid, with too many feet and a patterned gait, and the hair on the back of Toria's neck raised. She did not hold her breath but kept steady her inhales and exhales. If some sort of werecreature approached, skittering along the hallway in their alternate form, the sound of her heartbeat alone had already caught her.

Not a wolf, by the absence of clicking nails. A bear's steps would be more ponderous, and the odds of a feline werecreature in this part of Britannia were slim to none.

Except her magesight did not reveal the echo of any living creature.

The footsteps closed on Sarnai's former office until whatever stalked the building paused outside. A gentle thud hit the door, and it swung open. Toria wrapped her hand around the hilt of her rapier, ready to draw. She extended her opposite palm and drew energy into herself, preparing a concussive blast.

One of the four-legged robots nudged into the office. Toria relaxed her shoulders and lowered her hand. Dr. Reese had mentioned that his coworkers in the robotics department often let the prototype pack animals roam the property, allowing the learning computer programs to gather data on how to navigate unfamiliar terrain. The evening round-up must have missed one.

Even as she justified the robot's presence to herself, Toria could not miss how it had stopped in the office that contained an intruder. Or how the beast seemed to stare at her through nonexistent eyes.

Silly to anthropomorphize the robot. Her memory afforded the original prototypes Toria helped build during college too much precedence, when the group gave each one ridiculous nicknames and color schemes. These constructs were nothing like that, sleek with plain metallic plating.

It had no apparent face, but it might have a camera in the sensors that ringed the bulk of its body. Toria hated to destroy someone's work, but she could not risk discovery, even after the fact. Before she could leave the building and stroll off the premises, Toria would have to induce a power surge in the robot and fry the security camera a second time.

Except it could never be that easy, could it?

Toria hopped off the credenza and settled the satchel against her hip, patting the notebook contained within. "Easy, buddy," she said, sidling along the office wall until she paused next to the robot. "Sorry about this."

She was unsure whether she apologized more to the robot or to the poor scientist about to lose an expensive prototype. Toria lifted one hand.

The robot raised its fifth prehensile limb, mirroring her movement.

"I guess you can't make it easy for me either, huh?" She pulled power, and electricity crackled around her fingers, stirring the air currents in the office.

Three blades emerged from the robot's rubberized "paw." The curved, serrated edges glinted in the light from the hallway.

"Oh, hell." Toria twisted her body and summoned the most powerful shields she could, but the robot stood too close. Stripes of fire burned across her side, and she swallowed a scream of pain.

But too close worked both ways, and before it had a chance to swipe its claws in the opposite direction, Toria slapped both hands against its barrel-shaped torso and shoved raw power through it. The computer boards contained within could not handle that much electricity. The robot froze in place before toppling over.

Before it hit the ground, Toria had already sprinted halfway down the hall. Who knew how many more of those creatures roamed the property, inside and out? Pain sparked at her side with every step, the exposed wounds burning in the air.

She paused long enough to knock out the security camera before she fled the building and shot for the fence line. She bit her tongue against the pain in her side. Blood filled her mouth, and she spat.

Toria dropped her shields to conserve energy and vaulted the fence using a burst of supporting air. She hit the ground and staggered, the edges of her vision fuzzy. A spared moment of stillness showed no evidence of pursuit, so she stripped off the sheer blouse she wore over a camisole and wadded it against the blood seeping from her side. She tied the sleeves together to fix it in place.

She set off for the motorcycle, pain stabbing at every step, and hoped she made it to her ride without passing out. Hoped she was able to drive the thing without aggravating her wounds further. Hoped she made it to Kane's side, the safest place she knew.

But even with the distraction of pain, she knew how easy those robotic claws could have inflicted the wounds on Sarnai's body.

Kane waited for her at the front entrance to the country estate. Toria was surprised he hadn't sprinted down the lane the moment he sensed her approach.

The musk-scented leather jacket she found in the motorcycle's tank bag hid the bloodied mock bandage from the police. Darkness covered the streaks of blood that marred her dark-wash jeans. The officers on the evening security detail recognized her and let her pass without comment or close inspection.

Toria swung one leg off the motorcycle and staggered to the side, almost dropping the bike. But Kane was there, supporting the vehicle's weight until she could shove down the kickstand.

"What the hell did you do to yourself?" Kane rushed around the bike to wrap an arm around Toria. They left the bike behind as he half-helped, half-carried her into the house. "Where have you been?"

"Long story," Toria said, around teeth gritted against pain. "Both accounts."

Sharing the house with three werecreatures meant that Zhinu, Mrs. Hamilton, and Walter rushed into the foyer as soon as they scented the wound and blood. Zhinu gasped and covered her mouth as Toria dropped her shoulders to let the leather jacket fall to the floor

Mrs. Hamilton wasted no time assuming charge. "You can walk, girl?"

Toria grunted some sort of affirmation and allowed Kane to haul her along in Mrs. Hamilton's wake until they arrived in the kitchen. Walter pulled out a wooden chair from under a table in the cozy space, and it wasn't until Toria sank into it that she noted how much her hands quavered.

She didn't remember most of the ride home from the lab. A miracle she'd made it in one piece. But she was with Kane now. Kane would take care of her.

The thoughts came as if from a distance, and the more scientific portion of Toria's brain informed her that she was in shock. Pain seared her torso as Kane knelt and pulled a bit of the former blouse from her wound. Dried blood adhered the fabric to her skin. Her hands shot out, and she gripped the edge of the table, swallowing a curse.

"This should be fun." Kane rose to his feet and turned to Mrs. Hamilton. "Sounds cliché, but I will need clean water to separate this cloth from her skin."

"Hot?" Zhinu asked.

"Faster to heat it myself," Kane said. "Clean is what I'm more concerned about, to prevent introducing anything to cause infection. Well, anything else besides what might already be there."

"I've just the thing," Walter said. Everyone in the room, including his mother, jerked at the rare sound of his voice. "I keep filtered water for my fish tank. Will two jugs be enough?"

"Perfect," Kane said.

Walter lumbered out of the kitchen, and Mrs. Hamilton fetched a deep pan from a cupboard and set it on the table near Kane. When her son returned and poured the water, Kane pressed Zhinu into service to fetch clean cloth from Mrs. Hamilton's store of worn-out clothing, and he cut Toria's camisole away with kitchen scissors.

Embarrassment was the furthest thing from her mind, even wearing just her bra and surrounded by the others. The last of the adrenaline had worn off, and Toria *hurt*.

"I know, hon." Kane muttered further reassurances under his breath. He dipped his fingers in the pot of filtered water.

Toria gasped at the echo of power as her partner funneled energy into the liquid, heating it to steaming in seconds. The energy ripped through her as if he dragged glass shards along her insides. By the time this finished, her fingerprints would be embedded in the table.

"I already know I need stitches," she said, gasping around the words. "Knock me out already."

"Not until I see it." Kane used the clean water to soak her makeshift bandage, loosening the shirt and camisole fabric and unsticking it from her skin. "I might be able to do enough so that you don't need to get sewn up."

The Hamiltons had retreated to the other side of the kitchen, Mrs. Hamilton setting out items to make tea while Walter heated water the old-fashioned method via kettle and stove. Zhinu lurked nearby. She stared at the slow operation of Kane pulling away fabric, bit by bit. If anything, her presence goaded Toria into acting tougher than she felt at the moment. Hard to give in to tears when the concerned client hovered.

"Can you heal her?" Zhinu asked. "I saw Victory heal a wound on Mikelos' hand once. Can you do that for Toria?"

"It doesn't work the same way, but I'll see what I can do," Kane said, keeping his attention on Toria. "Tor, let me check your mobility."

She allowed him to manipulate her right arm, lifting and extending the limb in different directions. A glance at the exposed wounds showed four vertical gouges, stretching from her hip to the band of her bra. Not as much fresh blood welled from the deep scratches as she expected, but an invisible pressure against her side meant Kane had built a shield to keep them from splitting while he maneuvered her body how he wanted.

When he moved to her torso, she rested her head upon her crossed arms, half sprawled over the table to give Kane access to the injury without forcing her to hold her arms up. Toria's entire focus centered on the lines of fire along her side.

"I think I can close them most of the way," Kane said. "But you know it's going to hurt like crazy before it gets better. Or, I can numb the pain and stitch you up, let you heal the long way."

Toria grunted in acknowledgment. The easy way was so tempting. But the information gathered at the lab, Sarnai's notebook and the news about the violent robots, meant she could not afford to be out of fighting shape for the time needed until Kane could remove the stitches. Days versus more than a fortnight. "First option."

He knew her well enough not to ask whether she was sure. Instead, Kane said, "Zhinu and Walter. I need your help." Soon, Kane shoved a pillow under Toria's face while two sets of hands pulled her arms across the table. Zhinu and Walter each gripped one of her hands.

"Wait, wait," Toria said, almost pulling away from them.

"We know," Zhinu said. She patted Toria's hand. "We can handle it. You squeeze as hard as you need."

Because the werecreatures would heal in moments if she crushed their hands. Toria breathed deep. "Okay. Do it."

Kane settled a warm palm on either side of the wound, and Toria dropped every shred of her shielding, mental and physical. Between Kane's affinity as an earth mage and their magical bond, he could pour power into her. Knit the very fabric of her body together in moments.

But that amount of raw earth power clashed with her storm. His warm palms changed to clammy mud, and it was as if a landslide buffeted Toria from every angle. The roar of an earthquake drowned out the homey sounds of the kitchen, and even covered the bellow of pain she screamed into the pillow underneath her face. Pain overwhelmed every nerve ending, and with blissful relief, Toria passed out.

"Mail call." Kane perched on the arm of the sofa where Toria reclined and tossed a letter onto her lap.

She dropped her novel onto her blanket-covered legs and collected the thick envelope. When she flipped it over, Toria squealed in delight at the familiar handwriting, but a stab of pain reminded her that sitting up so quickly remained a terrible idea.

Instead, she hugged Liam's letter to her chest and asked, "You get something from Archer?"

"Yeah, a quick note." Kane patted his back pocket. "He's fine. Sends his love."

"Ugh, you can do better than that," Toria said. "Come sit with me. I'm bored."

"And whose fault is that?"

Her distraction peeling open the envelop saved Kane from a glare. He had confined Toria to forced relaxation for at least three days following the healing session. The gouges on her skin had closed over, leaving vertical blood-red lines across her torso. But the muscle beneath was a different story. Neither of them wanted her out of commission for too long.

Kane had related his encounter with Gan to Toria. Toria had shown him and Zhinu the notebook she stole from the labs. No word had come so far from Londinium, from Sarnai's father or any other members of his community. And the sheen that surrounded the notebook protected the contents from any attempt at deciphering them.

Sarnai's last set-spell had encoded the notebook, and the letters and symbols on the pages rearranged themselves every few seconds. But the seconds between grew more prolonged, so it was a matter of waiting out the spell. When it ran out of power, the code would stop switching. Kane proposed that the final product would not involve a cipher at all, but Sarnai had been a scientist, even if low level, and Toria understood how they thought.

It's what she would have done, after all.

So, a sort of stasis fell over the country estate. Zhinu couldn't leave. Toria couldn't move. And Kane refused to leave either of them unprotected.

Toria ripped open the final edge of the envelope and withdrew the contents. Three—no, four pages of Liam's cramped, precise script. She imagined him writing the letter at the desk next to her own in the loft apartment. Or maybe in his office at the anthropology department of Jarimis University, cluttered with books and papers.

She devoured the words, and returned to the top to read them a second time. Kane settled himself at the other end of the couch and didn't even complain when Toria shoved her feet in his lap.

When Toria lowered the pages, he asked, "Anything good?"

"He sends love to you, too," Toria said. "And says he misses me." A tension within her eased that she hadn't even known existed.

And her partner, who missed nothing, wrapped a firm hand around her bare foot. "You thought he wouldn't?"

"From his perspective, I've already been gone for such a long time. I guess I figured...." She plucked at the woven blanket. Firmer, she repeated, "I guess I figured he'd be used to it."

Kane's burst of laughter echoed through their suite. "You're a dummy sometimes. You know that?"

She resisted the urge to kick him. "Takes one to know one."

"But in this case, seriously," Kane said. "He's crazy about you. Archer said he got tired of the man drifting around the mage school looking pathetic."

"Yeah, Liam said Archer made him join the kids for game nights." An amusing mental image, of her respectable academic involved in the raucous board game evenings that tended to end with Archer devising ever more convoluted dares for his students to accomplish.

"Oh gods," Kane said. "He didn't tell me that. I wonder whether he let Liam come up with dares or made him do the same as the kids."

Either scenario was humorous, and Toria suppressed giggles because laughing hurt. "Stop," she said. "I can't handle it."

She had meant she could not handle laughing, but Kane dug a thumb into the pad of her foot until contentment—internal and pushed from her partner—swept from his touch throughout the rest of her body.

"Yes, you can." Kane rubbed her foot for another moment. He switched to the other, repeating his touch on the pressure points there.

"Doesn't mean I like it," Toria said. "I'm sorry that I never really thought about you being apart from Archer like this. Selfish of me."

"I don't think it was selfishness. More like a healthy amount of narcissism." Kane smoothed the blanket over Toria's feet but made no move to rise from the couch. "We're in each other's minds so much already. We don't need to know each other's every thought on top of it."

"And we shouldn't," Toria said. He might be the other half of her soul, but Kane was not the other half of her brain. They were separate people with different interests and relationships.

That did not stop them from knowing each other inside and out, as evident when Kane picked out her line of thinking. "We're not a single being."

"Lucky for that. Otherwise, I'd have to think mushrooms were an acceptable form of food."

"Mushrooms are delicious. You're the one who insists on acting like white chocolate is in any shape related to the real thing."

"All chocolate is the height of perfection," Toria said. That particular long-running debate would never resolve. "But seriously. How do you handle being away from Archer? I mean, I know you're not blind to the male form while we're out on the town."

Kane stared out the window into the blue afternoon sky. Toria did not rush his response, knowing he would give her a considered truth, not a trite reassurance.

Finally, he said, "Archer does not ask or expect blindness from me, nor I from him. He and I are not a single being either. We're partners, like you and me. But it's not as easy as being with you because we can't cheat. Requires more work, more communication."

"You hardly ever write when we're on contract." Most of the correspondence between Kane and Archer, when they worked in Europa, consisted of quick telegrams, far from private.

"Because we make a point to focus on the communication when I'm home," Kane said. "That's why I was so shocked you and Liam never discussed the status of your relationship before we left on contract."

"That's fair." Before her time with Liam, Toria had never experienced a serious relationship. Only one-night stands. Maybe one-weekend stands, a single week at the most, depending on the circumstances. Sex, not romance. She and Liam could do sex *and* romance. Even when the latter confused her more than anything else, she always ensured Liam knew she appreciated his effort. "Something for us to work on when we get home."

"Because he'll be there when you get home," Kane said. "Right?"

"Right."

They traded smiles, and Toria retrieved her book. Kane appeared content to drowse, still recovering from the power he expended in a single burst to heal her.

She loved being with him, out in the world, following the career they had chosen and trained for together. A decision made a decade ago, though, between the two of them against the world.

Not four.

After three days, boredom chased Kane to Londinium.

To be specific, the combined personality forces of Toria and Zhinu chased him to Londinium. The lack of word from the Chingis community beyond the brief visit from Gan frustrated and worried Zhinu. "You've developed a rapport with Gan," she said. "Visit him. Find out what you can."

From Toria, on the other hand, the prodding had involved a lot more bitching about his hovering. So, with the better part of valor, Kane returned to the townhouse in Londinium for a relaxed dinner with Rob before a mission of his own.

He had no specific address for Gan Baatar, but he did have the location of the Chingis community center-slash-house of worship from Zhinu. The mercenary bar sat about four blocks away, which explained Kane's initial run-in with him.

The community center was locked and dark, unsurprising at the late hour. Kane shoved his hands into his pockets and strolled in the direction of the bar, watching for Gan or anyone else with dark skin and tattoos.

Of course, that also worked as a description for himself, even if the skin tone was not quite a match and the tattoos less prolific.

A block away from the bar, Gan slipped out of the shadows and fell in step alongside Kane. In place of a greeting, he said, "What are you doing here, Nalamas?"

"Enjoying an evening out. Yourself?"

"This is my neighborhood. But you knew that already, didn't you?"

"Perhaps." Since the bar stood right there, Kane asked, "Care for a drink?"

"If you're buying."

Once inside, Gan led Kane to an empty booth. Far fewer people, obvious mercs or otherwise, crowded the room on a weeknight. Kane ordered from the passing waitress.

Kane and Gan stared at each other across the table. Kane assumed he should make the first move since he had entered Gan's territory, as it were. Ask about Gan's uncle, whether he'd made any more noise about going after Zhinu.

Instead, what came out of his mouth was, "Pick any pockets lately?"

Before Gan could respond, the waitress returned with their drinks. "Enjoy your evening, boys. Shout if you need anything."

"We will, thank you," Kane said. When he turned to Gan, his wallet sat on the table between them.

Gan sipped his beer as if he had no cares in the world.

Kane replaced his wallet in his pocket. If it surprised Gan when Kane didn't bother to check the contents, he didn't show it.

And, of course, credit where credit was due. "Nice lift," Kane said.

"Thanks." A new arrival in the bar drew Gan's attention, and he slid his beer across the table to Kane's side. "Don't say anything. This is about to get awkward."

A man who shared Gan's nose, and maybe the arc of his cheekbones, stormed to a halt at their table. The similarities ended there. He kept his hair cropped short, and Kane spotted no tattoos on the man's slim arms, though that did not discount ink elsewhere on his body.

He crossed those bare arms over this chest, though his youth and lanky frame diminished his aura of attempted menace. "Uncle says you have to come home now." He turned a scathing look upon Kane, the beers on the table, or perhaps both. "You're in for an ass-kicking if I tell him you're here."

"Tell Uncle I'll visit whenever I please, since I no longer live under his roof," Gan said. "Get out of here, Enku."

The table hid Gan's hands, but Kane could tell that he clenched his fists, whether in frustration or anger, from the stiff muscles in his arms, the tension in his shoulders. Kane knew little about Gan's culture beyond that gleaned from the news reports about Sarnai's death. But he did not appreciate bullies, and while Gan might be able to toss this kid across the room and didn't need Kane to stand up for him, Kane had never been one to sit back and wait out hate.

Toria would have already listed off half a dozen reasons the kid should leave them alone, with added commentary about personal freedoms and the virtues of a good drink. But his partner was not here, so Kane would have to pick up the slack. If Toria was the other half of his soul, it meant some of her attitude resided in himself, and while it was not comfortable, he had no problem pulling it out.

Kane lifted his beer for a long sip, enjoying the distaste that flashed across the newcomer's face. "I'm sure there's no rush for Enku to leave us. We're having fun." He forced the expression that never failed to pull Archer away from his work and into Kane's arms and directed its full force at the other man. "Plenty of room for three."

Points of color, from either embarrassment or terror, rose on Enku's cheeks. He opened his mouth once, twice, but no words came out. He glared at Gan once more before turning on his heel and fleeing the bar.

A choking noise across from Kane turned out to be Gan attempting to hold in laughter. Kane allowed his hilarity to spring free, and for two glorious moments, the men howled. Kane wiped away tears and pushed Gan's beer back to him. "I hope I didn't lay it on too thick."

"Are you kidding? That was perfect." Gan downed the last of his drink and nudged the empty glass to the end of the table. "It must have taken Enku a month's worth of courage to step foot in here. Now he'll never come back."

"Was it the alcohol or that you were in here with the likes of me?" Most people had trouble seeing beyond Kane's height and combat-ready physique, but Enku had noted Kane's insinuation with no problem. Toria would burst with pride when Kane relayed the encounter.

"My people tend to reserve alcohol for more ceremonial purposes," Gan said. "And there's no culture of condemning same-sex relationships among those back east, but lots of pressure to continue the family lines here in Britannia. I cemented my reputation when I refused to wed Sarnai for my own reasons, so I'm not worried that Enku is going to run home and whine about my new boyfriend."

Gan's words poured a bucket of ice water over Kane's head. "You know we're not—"

"I know, I know," Gan said, "but Enku doesn't know that, and that's the point."

"Got it." Kane also finished his beer, and another shadow fell over the table. Good timing. But when he turned to order refills from the waitress, two men loomed instead. Mercenaries, based on the sword at one man's hip and the scar bisecting the other's cheek. Neither appeared pleased, but the sneer on Scar's lips worried Kane the most.

He placed both hands flat on the table, wishing for a moment that he carried his scimitar. He'd left it behind at the townhouse for fear of scaring Gan off. "Can I help you, gentlemen?"

Scar's glare never wavered, but his companion pointed to Gan and said, "This one's nothing but trouble, and we don't need to put up with him bringing more of his folk around."

Gan kept his face lowered to the table. If Gan's spark of attitude had dimmed that quickly, this meant more trouble. Except it seemed Toria's borrowed sass had not fled Kane. And he would not let prejudiced bullies push him around, no matter the source. "We're sharing a drink. No trouble here."

"Let's just go, Nalamas," Gan said.

"Nalamas, eh?" Recognition broke Scar's glare. "You're one of them warrior-mages."

Kane didn't always appreciate the fame that came with his status, but perhaps it would work in their favor this evening. "That's right. Kane Nalamas, at your service."

"Thought your partner was a girl," Scar said.

Before Kane could respond, the first man broke in. "Look at his hair. Could be a girl." Both men smirked.

Flirting with them would not diffuse this situation. It might make it worse, in the sort of way that tended to involve violence. Kane swung his legs out from under the booth and rose to his feet. He didn't tower over them, instead topping Scar by about an inch, but his relative youth showed in contrast to how their bulk ran to fat instead of muscle. Kane braced for another insult to Gan, but their next comment targeted a different source.

The swordsman glared at Kane. "You're from Limani, right? Why come over here to snatch good-paying work from British mercs?"

No sense in trying to defend his current contract with sweet talk about history with the clients, or even worse, friendship with Zhinu and Rob. "Come on, Gan."

Kane slid past Scar, his goal to pay the bill at the bar and vacate the premises, but the other man grabbed his arm. "Got nothing to say to that, huh?"

"No, I don't." Kane studied the man's hand. More scars nicked at his knuckles. "Release me."

"Hey, none of that in here, now." The waitress bustled up, her previous friendliness replaced with nervous concern. "Why are you bothering the other customers?"

Scar kept his hand on Kane's arm, and Sword responded, "We're having a friendly conversation with our coworker from across the sea. You know how it is." Nothing friendly showed in the darkness that hooded his stare.

The waitress grabbed for Sword as if to pull him away, but he elbowed her away. Whether intentional or not, he caught her off-balance. She pitched to the side, and Gan grabbed her shoulder before she could fall.

Scar's fingers tightened. "Get your dirty hands off her."

Too far. Kane shifted his weight, using Scar's bulk against him, and twisted out of the other man's grip. Scar grunted, and Sword drew the short blade from this waist. He swung it around as Kane sank his heels into the floor and pulled magic from the ground. The energy in the room shifted, but not by him.

Two daggers shot toward the mercenaries and halted, hanging mid-air with their points against the men's necks. The long, slender blades emanated a silver glow, and the mercenaries froze.

Kane called up magesight, which confirmed his suspicion: the knives had no physical form, instead manifest from pure energy. He tracked the daggers' paths to Gan. The man sat in the booth, hands flat on the table. One of the tattoos on his right forearm shimmered and sparked, and Gan's natural aura faded as he funneled power into the spell.

Even Kane and Toria together could not create a physical object out of magical ether. These knives would fade in seconds, and Gan would have done nothing more than stoke the mercenaries' fury against them.

"Lower your weapon," Kane said. "And back away. No sudden movement. He won't hurt you."

The mercenaries followed directions, though their glares could melt steel, and the waitress scampered out of the field of fire.

"Drop the spell, Gan."

The daggers shimmered away as if they had never existed at all, and power flowed into the space with a muffled *whoomph* Kane suspected no one else sensed.

"We're leaving now," Kane said. Gan exited the booth and shook out his arm. The mercenaries flinched as one, but they allowed Gan and Kane to pass.

Once out on the street, Kane hauled Gan away from the bar by the wrist. Gan stumbled in Kane's wake, unresisting until they halted a few blocks away. Apartment buildings towered above the deserted street, as safe a place as any.

Kane released Gan and turned on him. Stabbed a finger at Gan's arm. "What the hell." Question, exclamation, however Gan decided to take it.

"Wasn't about to let them hurt the girl."

"They weren't going to hurt the girl!"

"Didn't know that."

"They were jerks, not assholes."

"What's the difference?"

Gan stood chest to chest with Kane, and his warm, beer-tinged breath burst in Kane's face. How had Kane ever found the stubborn idiot attractive? Even Toria, at her wildest, had better taste.

Kane centered himself. Stepped back. Asked the real question that had haunted him since Gan summoned, of all the damned things, flying knives. "Have you ever visited Foundry Labs?"

Confusion, then rage, darkened Gan's face. "You think I had something to do with Sarnai's death?"

"Something ripped her to shreds." Kane spread his hands as if presenting Gan's ink. "You showed one way it could have been possible."

The same sensation from the bar, of power drawn from the air, surged across Kane's skin. He backed away and raised his shields. He was no combat mage like Toria, couldn't throw lightning or shock opponents. But he was handy with knives himself, and he drew the short blade he kept strapped to the small of his back.

Didn't thrust it at Gan or make any threatening motions. But held it ready.

Even without magesight, a shiver of power roiled under Gan's skin. The man could summon knives. What other tricks did his ink hide?

Gan turned his back on Kane and sauntered away into the darkness, leaving Kane alone in the street. Relief swept through him. He had not wanted to fight. Wasn't sure he would win if he did.

Kane replaced his dagger and flipped his shirt over the sheath. No information was worthless, so he would not count this trip as a waste. But two brains were better than one, and he could use Toria's input on the newest wrinkle in this mystery.

Descending the stairs from the third to the first floor, where she intended to spend the afternoon with Zhinu, was absolute torture. Even with Walter's assistance.

She preferred to collapse onto the library couch, boneless from exhaustion, but her side already hurt enough from the short distance traveled. Instead, Walter eased her down while Zhinu fluttered about in concern.

If she stayed in her suite any longer, she would wear through Liam's letter from reading it over and over again. Obsessing was not healthy, but missing Liam overwhelmed any desire she had to read novels or meditate. Hence this excursion, where the afternoon sun brightened both the room and her mood. Zhinu readied her a cup of tea, heavy on the sugar.

"I feel like I should be contracting you," Toria said as she accepted the cup. "I'm not much of a bodyguard right now. You're providing all the protection."

Zhinu waved the morning paper. "Don't forget the entertainment."

"If I recall, entertainment was not written into the original protection contract."

"Yet you and Kane are so entertaining when you're together. A laugh a minute."

Toria chucked a throw pillow between the two couches that marked the library's sitting area. Zhinu threw it back at once but aimed it at the empty seat next to Toria so that she did not jostle her tea—or her side.

"What's in the news today?" Toria asked. "I've felt a bit cut off from the world while upstairs, now that Kane is in the city."

Zhinu shifted the tea tray aside and spread the newspaper across the low table between them. "I'm guessing you don't want to hear about the latest society gossip?"

"Not unless it's extra scandalous."

"Define scandalous. We've got descriptions of gowns and the handmade decorations at a lady's tea."

"Nothing about affairs that end with duels at dawn?"

"Not today." Zhinu flipped to the first page of the newspaper. "And the top headlines all involve the latest bill in Parliament. Something about funding issues and redistricting."

Toria sipped her tea. "Next."

"Oh, this is interesting. Two werepanthers and a werewolf hospitalized in Parisii."

"Huh," Toria said. The way werecreature healing worked, switching between forms, an injury had to be severe to force them into specialized care. "That is interesting. They give the reason for such a bad fight?"

"Not a fight at all, apparently. An illness."

"Ouch." Any bacteria or virus powerful enough to lay out werecreatures would knock humans, and even elves, flat.

Zhinu fed tidbits from the rest of the paper to Toria, but nothing dramatic had happened in the past twenty-four hours. The parliamentary season was off to a productive opening, crime was low, and interest rates were lower. An op-ed whined about funds allocated for social programs in Londinium, particularly those that benefited the Chingis community. Just another day in the British Empire.

Perhaps Kane's day was more interesting, but Toria sensed baseline health alone at his current distance, without even a blip to indicate heightened emotion.

With another round of tea, they enjoyed comfortable silence. Mrs. Hamilton called a question to her son in another part of the house. The clock chimed once.

"Time to recheck the notebook?" Zhinu asked.

"Oh gods, yes." Toria placed her teacup on the tray. "I'm so bored."

Zhinu fetched the notebook from a locked desk drawer and positioned it in front of Toria on the table. Between the newspaper and tea tray, the small book appeared innocuous. But when Toria called her magesight, the bundle of paper crawled with energy.

"Any change?" Zhinu hovered near Toria, as if ready to leap between her and any mystical trap the notebook might present.

Toria banished her extra-sensory ability, and the real world resumed its dull trappings. "Perhaps a bit dimmer? But the magic is still there. Whatever protective spell Sarnai Khan used, it's one of the most powerful I've ever seen to last this long past the caster's death."

She flipped open the cover, ignoring Zhinu's sharp gasp. Toria had carried the damned thing out of the lab and across what seemed like half the island while bleeding from multiple wounds. It would not hurt her now. But she could not decipher the jumbled mess of words and letters on the first page. And between one glance at Zhinu and her next examination of the page, the chaos had altered, letters switching places as if they had always been there. But today was a new day. Toria had made it all the way downstairs, after all. She could manage a more in-depth survey. "Do you mind locking the door? I'm going to do a deep-dive into the magical layers, and I don't want Mrs. Hamilton to distract me if she comes in." Toria folded the newspaper out of the way.

Zhinu didn't move. "Are you sure that's a good idea?"

"There are no such things as good ideas when mucking around with unfamiliar magic," Toria said. "But what have we got to lose?"

"We could lose you if there's a deeper trap there." But Zhinu crossed the library as she spoke. After she latched the library doors, she resumed her spot opposite Toria, hands clutched together.

"I'll be careful, I promise." Toria rested her fingertips on her thighs and grounded herself.

"You'd better. Or I'll never hear the end of it from Kane."

"If he has any voice left after he finishes with me." Toria shared a smile with Zhinu before shifting her attention to the notebook. Her magesight flicked into place.

The library, the ticking clock, Zhinu's aura—it all faded from Toria's consciousness until her entire being centered on the notebook. A collection of pages, cardstock binding, and the spiraled metal wire that held it all together. Magical energy suffused it all, but this time, Toria peered beyond the surface.

Despite her relative youth, Toria had experienced magic beyond the reasonable expectations of the mercenary lifestyle, even as a warrior-mage. Experienced a curse that cut her off from her power. Fought a mage who tried to manipulate her connection with Kane to steal their magical energy. Touched the magic of time itself. And yet, she had never before sensed anything like the power that encompassed this collection of notes.

Beyond the surface swirls of this magic, she found something more deep-rooted. A subtle pattern, shifting with unexpected movement, connecting and reconnecting like the most delicate circuit board. And try as she might, Toria could not read the magic. Couldn't anticipate the connections, couldn't comprehend how they worked to encode the notebook's writing.

To develop such a spell, Sarnai had to be one of the world's most powerful magic-users. But why would such a person work as an assistant at a tech lab? Even with the systemic racism that pervaded British culture, the last remaining magic school on the large island would have sensed such a talent and snatched her up for training. Unless Sarnai had not been the source of the power. Unless she had tapped into something more substantial.

Toria examined the bones of the set-spell with new eyes. For a split second, she considered the temptation to shield the notebook and freeze the decaying spell. She could bring the journal to the mages in Oxenafor and enlist their help to figure out the source of this unknown power. Toria's analytical mind longed to solve this mystery, to study how this magic worked, pick it apart, and learn how to put it together again.

But a woman had died, and the reason for that death might sit before her. If Toria preserved the spell, they would never decode the book. She would trade Sarnai's life, and Zhinu's freedom, for intellectual curiosity. Some knowledge was not worth obtaining.

With an internal sigh, Toria maneuvered out of the magic. The last of her magesight fell away as she lifted her tea, almost surprised to find her hand steady.

Zhinu waited for her to drink before asking, "Anything?"

How to explain the depths of what she had seen to someone with no context for how magic worked? "The spell is fading." But they already knew that.

"Well, time is finite," Zhinu said. "The spell will break. You will heal."

"You'll still be trapped in this house."

"I was trying not to think about that, thanks." Zhinu's soft tone muted the sting of her words.

Toria shifted on the couch, stretching limbs that tingled after her extended physical immobility. "But do you regret what you're missing right now? Luncheons and cocktail parties?"

"Not particularly. But I'd still prefer it be my choice."

A tentative knock sounded at the library door, and Zhinu answered it. Toria turned to the visitor as much as her torso allowed.

Mrs. Hamilton presented a folded paper to Zhinu. "Robert called a moment ago. He sends his love to you and a message for Ms. Connor." They discussed dinner plans, and Zhinu brought the note to Toria.

She opened it to reveal Mrs. Hamilton's neat script. "Oh, hell."

"What does he say?"

"Your husband will be here tomorrow afternoon to escort me to Foundry Laboratories. Dr. Tierney wants to speak to me."

Toria waited outside the estate's front door for Rob to arrive. A telephone call earlier that morning indicated he'd have enough time to collect her and turn around to get to their meeting with Dr. Tierney at the appointed time. When she had offered to drive herself and meet him there, the line had gone quiet for a moment. Then, the muffled sounds of the handset on the other end passed to a new person.

She had not been surprised when Kane responded to her offer. Her partner informed her in a tone that brooked no argument that it would not be best for her to arrive at the laboratory unescorted.

When Rob drove past the police, who continued to guard the estate's entrance, to collect her, Toria had expected stony silence. Not a kind greeting and queries regarding her healing, followed by a conversation in which Rob asked her educated opinion about whether to invest in another scientific pursuit. This one involved the use of graphene in fuel cells, and for a short time, Toria almost forgot their destination.

After a natural pause in the conversation, she poked the elephant that rode in the vehicle with them. "So, they know it was me?"

Rob answered with silence. When he finally answered, he kept his attention on the road. "They suspect, but they have no evidence. Something fried the security tape, and Dr. Tierney mentioned a sabotaged project. There aren't many storm mages in Britannia."

"There aren't many mages in Britannia, full stop."

"Then you understand the suspicion."

"What's our move?" If Rob had intended to throw Toria to the wolves, less than symbolic in this case, he had no reason to escort her on this visit. With one call to the police, those guarding the estate could have brought her without Rob ever leaving Londinium.

Rob caught at his bottom lip with his teeth for a moment, and said, "Kane assures me you have an excellent poker face, even when injured."

At that, she straightened in her seat. With a stretch of her power, she gathered from the ambient energy around them to reinforce a particular portion of her shielding. Not a trick she could maintain for long, and she would pay for it later with an enormous meal and passing out for at least eighteen hours. But for now, her pain receded until she could walk, and even run and fight, without distraction. "They won't even know I have a scratch."

Rob revealed no surprise when the security officer in the lobby informed him Dr. Tierney would be with them shortly, rather than waiting for them in the lobby herself. Toria followed his lead, from ignoring the dark expression the security officer shot her way to keeping quiet when Rob assured the guard that they were happy to wait for Dr. Tierney to finish her current meeting before she could speak with them.

But when the officer shut the office door behind them, Rob let out a gusty sigh that ended with a hint of a growl.

Toria refrained from comment as she settled into a seat next to Dr. Tierney's cluttered desk. The moments when Rob waited for anyone had to be few and far between now. And not by people under his employ.

While Rob paced, she studied the office décor. No matter the person, some hint of their personality shone through their workspace. Since her opinion of Dr.

Tierney was not stellar to begin with, she found no harm in snooping to find perhaps one thing they had in common beyond scientific interest.

Framed diplomas adorned one wall to the side of the desk. A large chalkboard dominated the opposite half of the office, featuring to-do lists, telephone numbers, and random notes. A lone birthday card stuck out of the top of the frame.

At home, Toria kept a handful of framed pictures on her desk. One of her with Kane soon after they bonded, a posed portrait with her parents at her college graduation, and a candid photo Archer snuck of her cuddling on a couch with Liam a few months ago. Archer's office at the mage school featured an entire bulletin board displaying dozens of pictures with her and Kane, with random students, and even artwork created by the younger kids. Liam's desk at the university held a single antique portrait of his adopted son, though frames with photos of other friends and family sprinkled his bookshelves.

Dr. Tierney's office contained a single photograph on her desk. A dozen men and women in military uniform, posing with thumbs up in front of a nondescript tent. Toria leaned forward to examine the uniform insignia. British armed forces, within the past five years or so based on the camouflage pattern worn, but the unit badges sparked no particular knowledge to her.

Rob stopped pacing long enough to glance at the picture she studied. "Huh. That's Squadron 17."

"You're familiar with every British military unit? Enough to recognize them by sight?" That seemed a bit neurotic, even for a werewolf.

"No, but it's easy enough to recognize the ones all killed tragically."

With that tidbit of information, Toria inspected the picture in a new light. Not a staged photo used in a magazine spread, but a personal candid. Which meant Dr. Tierney had to know one of the people in the image. Since the woman's position here at the lab had little to do with official military action, Toria asked the obvious. "How'd they die?"

Rob sat beside her. "Humanitarian mission to rural Bohem gone wrong. The Romans had intel about a terrorist cell operating in the area. When their spies informed on a military caravan traveling by night, Roman special forces attacked. Squadron 17 had been escorting two pregnant locals to better medical facilities."

"Roman special forces" often meant something like a lone vampire, maybe a pair of wereleopards. And a humanitarian mission was unlikely to have a werewolf escort so close to Roman territory. The British military was no joke, but Toria had seen first-hand what a single vampire could do at night even against armed humans. "No survivors?" she asked.

"The investigating team thinks the attack spared the two women. But they died of exposure within the next day or so."

"Shit."

"That's one way of putting it."

"Why would Tierney have a picture of them on her desk?"

"Good question," Rob said. "She may have been related to one of them."

"But as the only picture on her desk? That's a little weird. Kind of morbid."

Rob spread his hands. "You're the scientist. As far as I'm concerned, you're all a little weird."

They passed more time in silence until Rob straightened in his seat. High heels clicked in the hallway. The office door opened, and Dr. Tierney entered.

Rob did not stand to greet her, which spoke volumes about his opinion regarding this meeting. But Dr. Tierney didn't notice or didn't indicate she did. She deposited an armful of folders on her desk before shaking Rob's hand.

Both of them ignored Toria.

"Thank you for seeing me today, sir." Dr. Tierney sat at the edge of her desk chair, hands clasped on the wooden surface before her.

"I make it a point to remain accessible to all of those in my employ," Rob said. "Please consider the door to my office in Londinium always open."

Point one to Rob.

Dr. Tierney's face remained neutral. "This issue seemed important enough to require a personal touch. I'm sure you understand how the security measures we maintain at Foundry Laboratories ensure the value of our intellectual property."

Striking right in the purse strings. At least half a point to Tierney for that one.

But Rob was not the sort to play politics when already irritated. "Please explain to me what my wife's bodyguard has to do with this lab's intellectual property."

Now, Dr. Tierney flicked a glance to Toria. "You gave express permission for Ms. Connor to visit the labs during her personal time."

"Master Connor," said Rob, emphasizing Toria's formal title, "is a scientist in her own right, and I found no reason to deny her request."

Prey instinct stirred in Dr. Tierney, and she ducked her face to straighten a pile of paper on her desk to avoid his gaze.

When she didn't respond right away, Rob continued, "Is there a reason why you dragged me away from my busy schedule in the city, or did you merely wish to debate Master Connor's academic credentials?"

A flush darkened Dr. Tierney's neck, below her severe bun. "We have reason to believe that Master Connor broke into the laboratory and sabotaged an important robotics experiment."

More like the robotics experiment had attempted to sabotage Toria. This time, Toria awarded herself all the points for making no physical reaction to Dr. Tierney's version of events.

Rob also retained his composure at Dr. Tierney's words. "That is a serious allegation. I assume you have proof of this intrusion?"

"We do not."

"Then we're done here." Rob rose from his chair. "Thank you for your time, Dr. Tierney. We'll show ourselves out."

Dr. Tierney slammed her palms flat on her desk. "Wait!"

Toria paused halfway through rising. Rob turned around at the woman's exclamation. "Yes, Doctor?" he asked, voice mild.

The muscles in her jaw worked around clenched teeth. Finally, Dr. Tierney said, "Thank you for seeing me, your lordship."

Without a word, Rob motioned for Toria to follow him from the office. Once halfway down the hallway, she asked, "That should have been more of a fight."

"The good doctor knew she had nothing against you. But she doesn't know our relationship," Rob said. "If there had been a lack of friendship between us, I might have accepted her word at face value, without concern for proof. Perhaps the way I give Dr. Tierney such freedom to control the operation here needs revision."

Toria placed a hand against the door to the lobby before Rob could open it. With a voice pitched for Rob's ears alone, she said, "To be fair, she's right. I did break in. I did destroy a valuable piece of equipment."

"Out of a desire to help Zhinu," Rob said. "And for my wife's sake, I would have broken in with you."

Kane ached, a dull pain behind his left temple. Could be caffeine withdrawal. Could be the distance between him and Toria that always caused restless sleep.

Could be pure irritation at the man sprawled in the parlor of the Wallaces' Londinium home, his battered jeans and threadbare shirt in stark contrast to Kane's neat suit.

"Took you long enough to get back," Gan said.

Kane paused in the doorway and resisted the urge to press a palm to his aching head. He had spent the evening as an expensive, menacing accessory while Rob played poker and smoked cigars with fellow members of Parliament. The smoke always bothered him. "Should I frisk you before I toss you out?"

"I promise I didn't touch milord's silver." Gan unfolded himself and rose, arms outstretched. He spun in a slow circle as if in proof that his hip-hugging clothing hid no secrets.

Nope, headache due to the erstwhile—how did Kane categorize him? They were not friends. Gan was not a mage in the same way Kane was, but he did use magic.

So, a suspect.

Gan's smirk fell when Kane did not respond. His voice flat after his previous snark, he said, "You still think I had something to do with Sarnai's death."

"Yes." Gan's magical daggers could have caused the wounds. But how had he accessed the office where Sarnai worked, in such a secured facility? Even Toria's little escapade had not gone unnoticed. "No. I don't know."

Kane longed to pour himself a glass from the bar in the corner, but the alcohol would do him no good. Instead, he dropped into the seat opposite the one Gan had vacated and pressed his fingers to his temples. If he wanted to heal his headache, he had to do it the old-fashioned way: tea and sleep.

But Gan was here, and until Kane figured out why, sleep was not in the plan for the near future. The other man resumed his seat. Kane lowered his hands and asked, "Any news on your uncle? Is he still determined to pin his daughter's death on Lady Wallace?"

"Nice to know I'm not the only suspect. I haven't seen him myself, but family gossip says he's waiting for Lady Wallace to return to Londinium to make a stink about it."

"She's not coming back here until something develops in the case," Kane said. "Right now, there are too many factors at play. Better for her to stay somewhere safe until a few of them resolve."

"Too many factors," Gan said. "You mean too many suspects?"

Yes. Zhinu. Gan. The robots. Even Toria herself, thanks to her little stunt. And nothing for Kane to do here, while Toria and Zhinu worked on the notebook. Except....

This conversation deserved something more potent than tea, regardless of his headache. Kane stood and beelined for the bar. "Want a drink?"

"Hospitality for one of my kind at the home of a nobleman? Of course, I want a drink." Gan accepted the tumbler of scotch Kane offered him. "To what do I owe this honor?"

"The liquor is more for me." Kane resumed his seat, clinked glasses with Gan, and sipped his drink. "I'm about to interrogate you, and the subject matter raises bad memories."

"By all means," Gan said, "enjoy your liquid courage."

They stared at each other in silence, appreciating the scotch. A maid poked her head into the parlor, but Kane waved her off. He studied the vibrant patterns that swept across Gan's bare arms, forcing himself to confront long-buried memories.

A gaunt man in leather breeches and nothing else, his pale skin decorated with tattoos. Kane's fingers formed claws as he gripped the armrest. *The man*

116

sprawled next to a thick steel tube, where an exposed control panel sprouted wires and circuit boards. Being near the old missile sickened Kane, nausea that roiled his stomach and shortened his breath. The man controlled the weapon. In Kane's magesight, cords of power linked the control panel with a design of ink on the man's calf.

Kane clutched his dagger. Toria had knocked the man away from them, but it was up to him to sever the connection with the destructive weapon. All of Limani depended on him—

The scotch spread warmth through his stomach, and Kane's magesight showed no lines of power connecting Gan to an unseen weapon. Even the tattoos themselves differed from those of the mage from his youth. Gan's ink spread in delicate designs that evoked a looping language, the swirls of a flowering vine, or perhaps the wavering lines of a sweeping plain. Nothing like the harsh slashes on the man he had almost killed, blunt strands of ink forced beneath the skin for the sake of power alone.

Kane finished his scotch and said, "Tell me about your tattoos."

"That is not the interrogation I was expecting."

"I imagine not."

"Is there a reason for the question, or are you just curious?" Gan lifted the arm that did not hold his glass and flexed his forearm.

As much as Kane enjoyed the play of the parlor's low light against the man's muscles, he answered, "Not idle curiosity. There's a method to my madness."

Gan set his empty glass on the side table and rose, extending a hand to Kane. "I can do you one better."

"This isn't where you offer to let me inspect your ink in more detail, is it?" Even as he spoke, Kane grasped Gan's warm hand and allowed the other man to pull him to his feet.

"That might be enjoyable for both of us," Gan said, squeezing Kane's hand before releasing him with the barest flutter of fingers against his palm. "But you've made your commitment elsewhere clear. No, I'm bringing you to the source."

"Excuse me?"

"Go change out of that fancy suit. The best way for me to prove that I did not kill my cousin is to make you an expert on Chingis tattoos. We're getting you inked."

They strolled down the street, two nondescript men. A bit under-dressed for the neighborhood, but the late hour meant few passersby. Two blocks, then three, before Kane asked, "Where are we going, exactly?" His headache persisted, despite chugging a bottle of water in his room while changing clothes.

"The underground."

The subway system crossed every part of Londinium. The infrastructure project became necessary when the second-largest city on the planet could no longer rely on private vehicles with combustion engines. Now, those unable to afford private electric town-cars could still work and socialize beyond their neighborhoods' constraints.

Toria hated the underground, but Kane had no problem descending below street level at the nearest station. In this part of the city, the tiled floors and walls gleamed. Framed posters advertised theater productions and museum exhibits. He matched Gan's silence as they waited for the next passenger train.

A patrolman studied them, but Kane lifted his chin in acknowledgment, and the man passed them without incident. The train arrived a moment later, and they boarded before the officer could have second thoughts about their presence.

It probably helped that they were leaving the vicinity instead of arriving.

On the train, they selected two seats and sat shoulder-to-shoulder. Kane lifted his right wrist and turned his hand, tracing the elven runes there. "You know I already have tattoos. How is getting another going to prove anything about you?"

Gan ignored the question. "What does that one mean?"

Kane pointed out the separate names. "Torialanthas Connor. Archer Sophin. Syrisinia."

"Your partner, your lover, and…?"

"A friend." Once presumed dead, now back among the living. At least on this plane of existence. But that story was too complicated to tell, with Kane not clear on all the details himself. He touched his right shoulder. "And I have a pair of crossed swords on my shoulder blade." The tattoos represented memories and promises, and neither could ever be broken.

"Interesting," Gan said.

He did not explain the patterns across his own skin, and Kane refrained from asking. Let the man keep his secrets for now. If this errand did not satisfy what Kane needed to know, he could query outright.

Passengers boarded and disembarked at each stop. The clothing quality changed the farther they traveled from the Wallaces' neighborhood. People dressed for an evening out transitioned to those in janitorial and food service uniforms.

Finally, Gan said, "This is us," and led Kane off the train.

This station could have been in another country: cracked tiles, stained flooring. Tattered flyers for discount electronics and want ads for seasonal work. No security officers here. Kane climbed behind Gan up a broken escalator to street level.

"Thought we were visiting one of your community," Kane said as he stayed on Gan's heels through the patrons who spilled out of a loud bar. The intersection around the train station seemed to be the entertainment center of whatever section of Londinium they stood in, but side streets featured quiet row homes.

Gan slowed once they passed through the crowd so Kane could walk alongside him. "Tuya doesn't like most of us."

A warning trickle of nerves danced along Kane's spine. "Dare I ask why?"

"Nothing suspicious," Gan said. "She likes me." He ran a hand over the opposite arm as if the designs on his skin proved the statement.

They turned a corner and passed small single-family houses so close together that sometimes paint color alone indicated the transition between each residence. Gan waited for a bicycle to pass before leading Kane to the opposite side of the street. "Tuya says the community elders are too hidebound," Gan continued.

"People like your uncle?"

"Exactly. Men too concerned with holding on to old customs than living their current lives."

"Heritage can be important," Kane said. Even twenty years later, his foster mother Victory made sure to include an orange as part of his winter holiday gifts because his mother had done so while still alive.

"And we should keep the important parts, not pretend that we're an island. Or a fortress under siege."

The picture of Sarnai that Kane had seen showed a young woman in long sleeves, and he did not remember any ink on the cousin who had approached them in the bar. "Do all of your people have tattoos?"

"No," Gan said with a sharp shake of his head. "No culture is homogenous. Tuya keeps alive a particular tradition. She wanted me to apprentice to her, but even if I have the gift, I don't have the artistry."

Before Kane could ask what Gan meant, the other man turned up a walkway. The homes on either side boasted tiny front yards of manicured grass, but someone had transformed the entire space in front of this darkened house into a garden with a riotous array of flowers. Kane followed Gan onto a small porch, where ivy crept along the rails, and Gan knocked at the door.

Silence. He knocked again. Before Kane could point out the late hour or lack of light in the windows, the door swung open beneath Gan's hand.

The doorway framed a woman backlit by low light. Wrinkles lined her dark olive skin, but her broad shoulders did not stoop with age. Pink curlers wound through her hair. Rather than a comical visage, her penetrating glare combined with her hawk-like nose made Kane want to apologize for the intrusion, and he wasn't even the subject of her attention.

"Tuya!" Gan said, either oblivious to or ignoring his reception. "Looking lovely as always."

Lines of ink traced the woman's neck, incongruous above her bright, patterned housecoat. "Gan Baatar. Still haven't invested in a watch, I see."

"Time has no meaning where you're concerned because you are as radiant now as the day I first met you."

"I've known you since you were three, you brat." Now, Tuya broke into a wide grin and opened her arms. After she and Gan embraced, she asked, "Who's your friend?"

"Kane Nalamas," Gan said. "Please meet Tuya Setseg, the only Chingis skin artist in Londinium."

"A pleasure, ma'am," Kane said and extended his hand.

Instead of shaking it, Tuya tugged his wrist closer to examine the names that wound around it. "Not bad, but not elven work. They mean anything, or did you think the language looked nifty?"

Her comment surprised Kane, but Gan responded before he could figure out how to answer. "Be nice. He's not that sort."

Tuya sniffed but dropped Kane's hand and stepped away. "No visits, no calls, and you show up at my door in the middle of the night with a foreign mage?"

How did she know? Kane summoned his magesight, and a vibrant aura of shimmering bronze swirled around Tuya. Water mages tended more toward blues and gold, but he had spent enough time around Archer to recognize her magic.

If the woman noted his inspection, she showed no sign. "You might as well come in. I'll put tea on."

Kane followed Gan into the house. He expected a cramped interior, the small house stuffed with the detritus of years. Instead, Tuya maintained a spare sense of style at odds with the vibrant garden out front. The parlor held furniture with clean lines, and art prints of subtle patterns provided spots of color along the walls. Rather than sterility, the kitchen they entered carried the scents of herbs and earthiness from the pots that lined the counters, which enveloped Kane like a warm comforter.

Tuya invited them to settle at the table, and she and Gan maintained a constant stream of chatter regarding local gossip. After she handed them steaming mugs, she disappeared elsewhere into the house.

Kane broke his silence and said, "I like her."

"Knew you would."

They sipped their tea, a tasty masala chai blend. Kane made a mental note to ask Tuya where she got her tea because Zhinu would adore it. Before he could ask Gan whether Tuya mixed it herself, Tuya bustled into the room.

She had changed into loose pants with a tank top and covered the plastic curlers with a scarf. But her clothing's plain fabric paled against the vibrant patterns that crossed her arms and even poked above the neckline of her shirt. If this was the woman responsible for Gan's tattoos, no wonder he brought Kane right to the source rather than answer any questions himself.

Tuya's gaze darted between them. "Not that I don't appreciate the visit, but it's time you boys told me what you're doing here."

Gan pointed to Kane. "My friend here needs a tattoo."

The mug slipped in Kane's hand, rattling on the table.

"But this man already has magic," Tuya said. "Why does he need more?"

"He doesn't need more. He needs to understand."

Kane broke in. "Understand what?"

"Why my tattoos mean I didn't kill my cousin," Gan said. He rested his hands flat on the table.

Kane mirrored his pose, their fingers inches apart on the aged wooden surface. "That doesn't make any sense."

They stared at each other. But the tension had nothing to do with flirtatiousness. The world beyond faded away, and neither man reacted when Tuya rose and exited the kitchen.

Breaking the silence, Gan asked, "Do you trust me?"

Kane bit his tongue on an immediate response. The question deserved more than a quippy answer. He shouldn't trust Gan. A man he barely knew, who was too involved with the matter of his cousin's death—the death that stood between his client and freedom. He had no reason to trust him.

But he had followed Gan to this house on the outskirts of Londinium. Shared tea that had made his headache vanish. He broke Gan's gaze and summoned magesight. A check around the room showed nothing dark about this place. Serenity permeated the kitchen, and even Gan seemed softer here under the warm lamplight.

Kane dismissed the magesight. "Yeah. I trust you." Besides, even if he hated it, it would be the work of moments to erase and heal the tattooed skin with his earth magic's innate healing ability. He had already done that once when the design around his wrist had come out crooked the first time.

"Let's go."

Kane followed Gan up a flight of stairs to a small landing surrounded by closed doors. Gan chose the one on the left, revealing a room that could have doubled as a meditation space or the sort of area that spas provided for massage therapy. Tuya even kneeled next to a pallet on the floor.

It resembled none of the other places Kane and Toria had received their tattoos. No samples of artwork and designs covered the walls—no blaring rock music like the shop in New Angouleme, which had drowned out the tattoo machines.

Instead, a water fountain tinkled in the corner, and more plants lined the windowsills. Tuya motioned him closer, and Kane folded his tall form into a kneeling position atop the pallet.

Awkwardness rippled through Kane. "So, do I get to pick out the tattoo?" A tall cabinet sat in one corner, so maybe Tuya did have a sketchpad or book of designs he could peruse. They would have to raise the lights in the wall sconces, which right now emanated less light than candles.

Tuya laughed, a light peal at odds with her solid frame.

When Kane looked to Gan for backup, the other man smirked. "Not how it works, I'm afraid."

"Please stretch out and relax," Tuya said, patting the empty mat.

After Kane did as instructed, stretching flat until his head rested on the soft pillow at one end, but his booted feet stayed on the wooden floor at the other, Tuya regained her feet. Kane caught glimpses of the woman bustling around the room from his prone position as she gathered supplies from the corner cabinet and instructed Gan to fetch her another mat from the hall closet.

"My knees aren't getting any younger," she said.

Gan returned with the requested mat and a pillow for himself. He arranged the rug to Tuya's specifications and settled himself out of the way.

Tuya returned to her position at Kane's side. But instead of turning to her supplies, she rested her hands atop her thighs and closed her eyes.

Once again, Kane called upon his magesight. Metallic tendrils of Tuya's aura spread from her body and crept through the air, imbuing the room with magic and Kane with calm. Magic worked through intent, and Kane read no harm in the power that investigated his shields.

He closed his eyes, dropping magesight and all but his most passive shields. Tuya must have sensed his acceptance of her magic because a low chant spilled from her mouth. Kane did not comprehend the words, which must be from her homeland. Gan echoed a handful of the phrases, but the power belonged to Tuya.

Her fingers brushed Kane's arm, but he did not react in surprise. He kept his body relaxed, allowing Tuya to circle Kane's wrist with strong fingers and pull his arm closer.

The chanting continued as she ran her hands along his bare skin, the pads of her fingers warm, with the barest hints of callous. Gravity no longer tethered Kane's body to the mat below him. Instead, a sort of light euphoria swept through him, as if he might float away at any moment.

Drugs in the tea? Within the air, which contained a hint of incense?

He kept his eyes closed as the magic in the air subsumed his body, as calm as if Archer's arms encircled him.

A tiny prick touched his arm. Sharp, but almost painless. It reminded Kane of an acupuncture session a handful of years ago, on some whim of Toria's. Was this the tattoo?

Kane wanted to ask questions. Why had Tuya chosen the inside of his forearm? What would be the design? How long would this take?

Instead, sleep washed over him.

Toria ignored Zhinu's yawn. Sleep was the furthest thing from her mind. She turned the next page in the notebook and stared at it, counting down from one minute.

Her eyeballs burned, but she resisted the urge to blink. At any moment, the letters and numbers on the page could swirl, or jump, or switch places, and Toria would have re-start the countdown over again.

But nothing changed. Sarnai's code remained in place as if Toria held a regular notebook. She rubbed her face, clearing the grit from her eyes with her knuckles. "That's ten pages."

Zhinu jerked to alertness. "You did it?"

"I didn't do anything," Toria said. "This notebook still holds power, but whatever spell caused the pages to change seems to have faded."

She flipped to the previous page, but the first line remained unchanged. Toria put the notebook on the desk in front of her and stroked the inside of her right forearm. The muscle there ached. Had she been so tense, clutching the book?

Zhinu left the couch to peer at the notebook over Toria's shoulder. "And that means we can decode it?" She curled her hands over Toria's shoulders and dug her thumbs into the stiff tension that made up Toria's neck.

Toria did not bother to stifle the groan that escaped her lips. "You have about a million years to stop doing that." She let her head drop forward, and the notebook blurred as her eyes crossed.

Zhinu worked on the knots in Toria's shoulders and neck for a few minutes, and the clock in the hall outside the library chimed one o'clock. "As much as I know you want to keep working," Zhinu said, "we should wait until morning for the next phase of this project. What's wrong with your arm?"

Toria hadn't even noticed scratching at it. Red lines from her nails stood out against her skin. "Huh. I have no idea. It feels weird." She squeezed her hand closed to resist the urge to keep itching. Zhinu stopped kneading her muscles, and both of them stared at her arm, Zhinu's long black hair falling in a curtain onto Toria's shoulder as she leaned forward.

Now that she had scratched at it, the soreness morphed into a prickling sensation. The impression localized to a section of her inner arm, but no other visual cues emerged as the scratches faded—no rash of any sort.

"Another protective spell set on the notebook?" Zhinu asked.

Toria flicked on her magesight, but no tendrils of magic stretched from the book to her arm or anywhere else. It sat unmoving, enveloped by a silver sheen. "I don't think so. Give me a second." She concentrated on her arm, penetrating with her magesight below her levels of shielding and into her body itself.

A smear of evergreen flickered. Toria sensed Kane within the bit of magic, along with something unfamiliar. A touch of pressure, a spark of pain that vanished as soon as it appeared. Kane was too far away for her to get a sense for more than his baseline condition, but no worry or fear echoed through their stretched link.

Whatever was wrong with her arm, Kane had something to do with it. But if he felt no concern, she would try to put it out of her mind.

And avoid scratching at it like a cluster of annoying mosquito bites. "My crazy partner is up to something, but I can't tell what." Toria patted Zhinu's hand. "You should sleep."

"And let you work yourself to exhaustion? Not likely." Zhinu pushed the notebook away from Toria and pulled her entire chair away from the table.

"Don't forget that we're both up to our necks in this now," Toria said. She crossed her arms as Zhinu locked the notebook away in her desk. "The police still haven't cleared you of Sarnai's murder. Dr. Tierney suspects me of—something. We can't afford to waste any time."

"And we can't afford to make stupid mistakes because we're exhausted." Zhinu pulled Toria out of the chair and led her from the library. "I'll leave a note for Mrs. Hamilton to have her wake us for breakfast. We can get to work bright and early."

Curse Zhinu's logic. Toria did not resist when pushed toward the stairs, in the direction of her suite. As much as the code tempted her with its secrets, the softness of her bed called as well.

But first, she'd better wrap her arm with a scarf so she didn't scratch herself raw in her sleep. What the hell was Kane up to?

The world returned to Kane in drips and drabs. Freshness suffused him, as if he had slept for longer than the few hours he'd managed the past few nights. But when his sight grew accustomed to the room's lighting, he found that the dimness came not from thick curtains but from the night that still cloaked the sky. Unless—

Kane jerked upright. Had he slept the day away? He would be missed, and he didn't dare imagine what alert Rob might have put out when he discovered his bodyguard missing.

A hand landed on Kane's shoulder. Gan crouched next to him. "Relax, man. I know it feels like more, but you've slept around two hours."

Before Kane could respond, Tuya bustled into the room. Her housecoat hung open over her comfortable clothing. "Finally awake, are we?" With the slide of a finger, the dimmer switch next to the door increased the room's lighting enough that Kane did not have to squint.

Gan moved his hand from Kane's shoulder to his wrist, lifting Kane's arm. "Look."

Kane's breath caught. A stylized tree in stark black decorated his forearm, no more than a hand-length long. Branches swept up to his elbow, and a widespread root cluster twined toward the names on his wrist. It was as if Tuya had plucked the design he would have chosen for himself right from Kane's mind, a pattern he had not even known he would love until he found it inked into his skin. He tore his attention away from the tattoo. "It's stunning. Thank you."

"You're welcome," she said, in the manner of a woman adept at accepting compliments that honored her skill. "The rest is up to you. Even I don't know what the final result will be."

Right. Because somehow, this tattoo was more than a pretty picture. Magesight showed him a swirl of energy beneath the surface of his skin, but the ripple of ink came from his imagination alone. If he couldn't interrogate Tuya about what the design did, he did need to ask, "Regular after-care instructions?"

Gan snickered. "Does it look like it needs care?"

His arm displayed nothing of what he remembered from his previous tattoos. Kane drew his fingers across the expanse of skin. It was as if the design had existed for months, or even years, already. The ink perhaps a bit more vibrant than the elven runes around his wrist, but the skin seemed healed otherwise.

"That's the perk of working on an earth mage," Tuya said, as Gan hauled Kane to his feet. "I manipulate your magic to embed the design and also to heal behind me. Otherwise, the excess power gets a little—" She fluttered her fingers. "Wonky."

The blood rushed from Kane's head, and Gan caught him before he could stumble. Now, the signs of power loss burst in his awareness as his stomach rumbled loud enough that they might have heard it two houses away—time for a second dinner, with perhaps extra helpings of dessert.

Tuya escorted them to her front door. "Gan, take him off for a full meal and let me get to bed. And next time you plan to visit with a strange mage, give a lady a call first. Just make sure he's as handsome as this one."

Kane blushed, but as they made their farewells, Tuya embraced him in a tight hug as affectionate as the one she gave Gan. Rising on her tiptoes, she whispered into his ear, "A pleasure to work with you, Kane."

"Thank you, Madame Tuya." And he meant it, even as he itched to explore the power that simmered beneath his skin.

But first, food. Gan brought them to an all-night diner a few blocks away, and he nursed a mug of coffee while Kane packed away two omelets and a stack of pancakes. He even managed a one-sided conversation about the local rugby league, not minding when Kane returned single-word responses between bites.

His appetite assuaged after a final strip of sausage, Kane pushed away his empty plate. "I hope this tattoo doesn't just allow me to eat as much as I want without gaining weight. Because regular magic use takes care of that for me."

"I promise that's not it," Gan said. "Because I've eaten twice as much after a long session."

They paid and exited the diner. "Where to now?" Kane asked. He knew better than to experiment with strange magic in an unshielded area. But it seemed unlikely Gan would have access to the type of workspace Kane used back home, based on off-hand comments about his shoebox apartment and the awkward relationship he maintained with the Chingis community.

Gan paused at the stairs down to the subway, examining the large city map decorated with colorful transit lines. "You're an earth mage, right? Will a giant park do?"

An ample green space would work as a second choice. "As long as it's deserted this late at night," Kane said. "And the wilder, the better." He preferred natural woods to a manicured garden, but Gan's knowledge of Londinium trumped Kane's, even after many visits to the city throughout his career.

"I know the perfect spot."

A short train ride brought them to another section of the city, and the stairs to the surface led them right to the entrance of Londinium's largest park. And the term "park" was a misnomer when he could stand in the center of the space and not sense that city surrounded him. With his sensitivity to the harm that urban areas inflicted on the earth, even Kane could drop combat-level shielding here and *breathe*.

Kane and Gan meandered through the darkness, in a companionable silence that seemed to suit the pre-dawn hour. At some point, Gan must have realized that he no longer played the leader. "You've been here before?"

"Once," Kane said. "Londinium's mage school used to own a section of the land here." The decline of mages meant that, like so many magical academies, the school retracted much of the power it used to enjoy. Last Kane knew, Londinium's mages had retreated to the college they maintained in Oxenafor.

They approached a wooded area that might fool most into assuming the land had been untouched for centuries. At least the school deeded the property to the city to remain parkland, not be developed by some corporation. Kane circled the thicket until he spotted the game trail that led deeper into the trees. "Come on," he said, stretching a hand behind him. Gan grasped it and followed Kane into the darkness.

They emerged into a clearing, too round to be natural. If stones once marked the points and arcs of a ritual circle, they had long since vanished. The new owners had allowed the area to return to its natural state—or as much as it could. The grass remained short and lush, remnants of a spell that would require decades or more to fade.

After directing Gan to the edge of the space, Kane stepped into the clearing. He centered himself and asked, "What do I do now?"

"It's part of you," Gan said. "Listen."

He and Toria did not often use ritual magic, eschewing such trappings for the shortcuts their bond allowed. But their teachers had insisted they learn, and it had come in handy more than once in assisting the handful of earth-aligned students at Limani's mage school. Kane settled onto the grass, cross-legged, and grounded himself. He did not need magesight to peer within himself, to delve into the magic that was part and parcel of his being.

129

But no matter how much he sought, beginning at his forearm and searching outward in expanding circles, he found no strange magic. As if he'd always had the tattoo.

Then, he remembered Gan's words. If the tattoo was part of him, it would not be unfamiliar. He searched for new, instead.

Seeking power seemed to awaken something new inside of him. His passive shields warped, but before he could panic, they stretched into the earth below him. He often had to filter the immense power of earth for effective use, even more so in the miasma of an urban center. Now, however, tendrils of magic immersed him with no effort on his part as they flowed into him.

All of his energy reserves topped off, and his shields grew to full strength. And a bright spot of happiness hovered at the edge of his consciousness. Toria? Did she sense the power that surged through him, even from miles away?

No. The sparking energy had a distinctive male presence. For a joyful moment, Kane imagined connecting with Archer across an entire ocean. That his other partner stood next to him, soaking in the offshoots of energy.

Reality intruded, and Kane sensed all at once that it was not Archer. The mote of power alongside him was Gan.

Instead of dismay, Kane reveled in the delight of touching Gan's inner self. The power of Tuya's art connected them, the magic at once unfamiliar and yet no different than any of the other energy Kane had ever manipulated. For all of Gan's tough-guy image, he was a jumbled ball of impish mischievousness. One who might pick the pocket of a rich man, or even just someone who pissed him off.

But no murderer.

Gan exhibited none of the darkness that tainted Kane. Each death he had ever dealt left a mark on his soul, his being, no matter how righteous.

Kane broke away from the magic before it could surge further, not wanting to blast a beacon of presence to every energy-sensitive being in Londinium. If he was honest with himself, he did not want to risk exposing his inner self to Gan longer than necessary. To show Gan the darkness he had done so much to prove he did not carry himself.

Kane opened eyes he hadn't known he had closed.

Across the clearing, Gan leaned against a tree. Despite the darkness, the glint of his teeth betrayed the delight on his face. "Understand now?"

His happiness was infectious. "Yes," Kane said.

Gan shoved away from his tree and entered the clearing. Once on his feet, Kane tugged Gan into a hug. The other man was no killer. Gan had been right, and the connection between them via Tuya's power proved it.

As if thinking of her summoned it, a final surge of energy arced between them. Kane kissed Gan. Or did Gan kiss him? For a brief moment, their lips met—a point of connection that seemed natural as Gan's lithe body pressed along his.

Kane jerked, extracting himself from Gan's grip but careful not to shove the other man away. "Shit. I'm sorry. That wasn't supposed to happen." Even if Gan had initiated the kiss, Kane had returned it, and that was on him.

But Gan had retreated at the same instant. "No, I'm sorry. Let the moment get away from me."

The joyfulness of Kane's brush with the earth beneath him soured as if a touch of urban decay had slipped in along with the pure elemental energy. Now, miles might have separated him from Gan. "I should get back," Kane said. "It's late."

An understatement. Purple streaked the sky as dawn pushed aside the night. The Wallace household would soon wake, and he did not want Rob to wonder after his erstwhile bodyguard.

They trekked out of the park and to the subway station, a new awkwardness between them tainting the previous easy camaraderie. Gan departed for another track with nothing more than a brief wave, his destination in the opposite direction of the exclusive neighborhood where generations of Wallaces had lived.

As he waited for his train, Kane rubbed the design on his forearm. He had no idea who had initiated the kiss, or if it had just been one of those things—the sort of thing he usually would discuss with Toria.

Except the tattoo itself would cause plenty of discussion on its own, and he'd better figure out how to explain that, first.

Toria squinted over the table, laden with the breakfast cooked by Mrs. Hamilton. She wasn't sure which was brighter—the sunlight pouring through the windows or Zhinu's expression of delight. Toria clutched her coffee mug. "It's too early."

"Too early for what?" Zhinu asked as she selected a strip of bacon from the plate between them.

"Everything." Strange dreams had haunted Toria, leaving her as restless as if she had not slept at all. Though her forearm no longer itched, she'd experienced an odd moment when she woke where the bare skin seemed—empty, almost. Covering the expanse of skin with a long-sleeved shirt fixed the weird sense of disassociation. "The guys are returning today."

"They are indeed." Zhinu made no effort to hide her pleasure at the fact. "You'll let me know when they're close?"

Newlyweds. Toria agreed, and rewarded herself with a berry-filled pastry when she resisted the urge to tease her friend. These days, she'd do the same in Zhinu's shoes if Liam were due to arrive at any moment.

After breakfast, Toria retired to the library to resume work on Sarnai's notebook. Zhinu promised to be downstairs to help as soon as possible, but Toria found no reason to wait. The first task was to copy the writing from the pages of the notebook onto fresh paper. Between Toria's scientific bent and Zhinu's facility with languages, they would attempt to decipher Sarnai's coded writing.

The work progressed throughout the morning. Mrs. Hamilton kept them supplied with fresh coffee, and Toria and Zhinu discarded a dozen coded possibilities and their variants. By the time Toria's shaky hands informed her that she needed another helping of solid food before more caffeine, a burst of contentment shivered under her skin. Kane neared the estate.

She warned Zhinu, as promised, laughing when the woman squealed in glee and raced for the front door. Toria followed at a steadier pace, but when Kane and Rob arrived at the entrance, she accepted Kane's embrace.

"We need to talk soon," Kane said, his words muffled by her hair. When Toria pulled away, Kane's face revealed nothing, and the emotion that leaked through their connection leaned more toward nerves than fear.

Rob insisted they share a civilized lunch while Toria and Zhinu updated the men on their work with Sarnai's notebook. Throughout the meal, Toria sensed Kane withholding something. Instead of launching into the decoding project right away once they finished eating, Toria followed Kane upstairs. As she locked the suite door behind her, Toria said, "You feel off. What's up?"

Kane wandered across the room and halted before the cold fireplace. In lieu of words, he tugged his right sleeve up, baring his forearm. The tree, with extensive branch and root system, stood out even against his dark skin.

"You got a tattoo?" Why would that cause such nervousness on his part? Both of their previous tattoos had been joint ventures, but Kane's skin belonged to no one but himself. She had no say in how he chose to adorn or modify it.

After so many years, some of their conversations needed no words. Toria crossed the room to examine her partner's new décor. She ran a finger along his smooth skin.

She froze. It was no traditional tattoo. "Don't tell me this is—"

"It is."

Toria released Kane's arm. Backed away. Breathed deep against the roar of blood in her ears. "What the fuck, Kane." Now last night's dreams made sense, and she scratched at her forearm through the cotton of her sleeve.

"Gan proved to me that he had nothing to do with his cousin's death." Kane kept his arms steady at this side. "We're connected through the magic. I saw inside him. And my soul is a hell of a lot darker than Gan's could ever be."

She forced herself to stop worrying at her forearm by wrapping her arms around her stomach. "And now you're connected to the man who tortured us when the Romans invaded Limani? Can he see inside you, too?" The tattooed mage who almost severed the bond between Toria and Kane, locking Toria away from her magic. The man who had manipulated the devastating power in a weapon from the Last War, threatening her home and everything she held dear.

They should have killed him when they had the chance. How young and naïve she had once been, to value the life of such a dangerous man after the damage he had wrought.

If Kane's soul carried darkness, she bore matching stains. A vision flooded her mind. Not her memory because she crouched at the edge of the scene. The tattooed mage from her nightmares dominated the field of view, and Kane's own hands wielded a blade that slid into the man's skin.

Toria banished the shared memory before the blood spilled. "What's that supposed to show me? That the only way to separate you from that power is to slice you open?"

Kane's fist balled. "No, damn it. The power is mine. The tattoo works as a channel. Like a set-spell prepared ahead of time. The power of the artist who created it is what links Gan and me. Not to that asshole from our past. Open your eyes, Toria."

Her partner meant it as a metaphor, but Toria had never needed an invitation to view Kane through magesight. With a mental twist, the magic of the surrounding world snapped into view. Kane's aura, a swirling mass of forest and evergreen, overwhelmed the surrounding ambient power.

And he was no different than she remembered. As if knowing what she sought, Kane bared his forearm to her. Nothing marred his familiar power—no taint of invasive energy. If anything, a knot of magic clustered where the new tattoo touched his skin, but the magic belonged to Kane alone. He had called it right by invoking the analogy of a set-spell. His arm blurred with the intensity she equated with material objects of power.

She crossed the space between them and gripped Kane's extended hand. "Drop your shields."

Without a moment's hesitation, he did as ordered. And because no matter what, Toria trusted Kane with every part of her herself, she did the same. They needed no physical connection, though the points where their skin met allowed her to dive into Kane's power with the ease of rain permeating topsoil.

She tunneled through Kane's magical makeup to seek any evidence of unnatural taint, any sign that Gan or this unknown tattooist had inserted a hidden trap within Kane's energy. He waited with infinite patience as she searched each virtual nook and cranny, sifting through familiar power.

Nothing. Kane remained wholly himself. And when she steeled herself to investigate the energy centered on the new tattoo, she found the same. Her partner spoke true. The power allowed him to filter magic with ease, even more so than when they worked together. As far as Kane was concerned, the tattoo allowed him to manipulate magic as if Toria always stood by his side.

Closer to her, rather than divided.

With the same hesitancy that always accompanied returning to her mind, separating bits of her soul connected with Kane, Toria settled into her skin. She bit her bottom lip against the words in her throat.

Kane heard them anyway, the silent acknowledgment that he was right. He allowed her stubbornness as much as he welcomed how she fit her body against his and held her close. They clung together, a step outside the real world for a handful of stolen moments.

Kane pressed a kiss to Toria's hair. "Ready to show me your progress on Sarnai's notebook?"

Toria withdrew from his embrace. "Yeah. You're the wordy one. I'm better with numbers. Let me update you on what Zhinu and I have done so far."

Toria worked with Kane and Zhinu late into the night, while Rob conducted his own business in another corner of the library. Despite easy conversation and the occasional joke, strain permeated the atmosphere as the three exchanged notes, consulted on new attempts, and puzzled out Sarnai's cramped handwriting.

Mrs. Hamilton forced them to leave the library for dinner. They gathered in the dining room for filling stew, accompanied by the fresh-pressed juice she delivered despite the resounding request for more coffee.

Toria traced designs in the condensation on the outside of her glass. "I feel like we're getting nowhere."

"At least we're not going backward," Kane said. "You two did good work eliminating a lot of possibilities."

Zhinu dipped a roll in her stew. "Ever the optimist, my friend."

"Are you sure there's nothing I can do to help?" Rob asked. "I know we don't want too many cooks in the kitchen, but I'm sure I can summon some contacts with experience in linguistics."

"But it's not another language," Toria said. "It's Loquella, I'm sure of it."

The common language of most of Europa might not have been Sarnai's first tongue, but she used no glyphs that signified the writing from her people's homeland to the east. Besides, the woman had been a scientist, trained to use Loquella as the language often used in conjunction with the physical arts of mathematics, physics, and chemistry.

But even Toria had to admit none of them had extensive experience in code-breaking.

After eating, they resumed the work. Rob packed away his papers first, and Zhinu soon followed him to bed. Kane lasted another hour before begging off as well.

"I'm going to work a bit more," Toria said, flipping through the notes Zhinu left her.

Kane paused alongside the table where Toria sat amidst scraps of discarded paper. He plucked the pen from behind her ear and buried his hands in her hair. Despite the low-key anxiety that pushed her to keep working, she leaned into Kane's touch as he dug his fingers into the pressure points at the base of her skull.

"Promise you're not avoiding me because you're mad about the tattoo?" Kane asked.

"You fight dirty." Toria pulled away from his hands with great reluctance, knowing that if she followed her partner upstairs, he would be more than willing to continue the massage and work the kinks from her shoulders. "But you had a weird night last night. Go pass out in a familiar bed. I do want to keep working on this."

She tilted back and accepted Kane's kiss on her cheek. When she did call it for the night, she would crawl into Kane's bed instead of her own. After their earlier spat, his unspoken neediness required tending, and a night snuggled against a warm body sounded like heaven.

But as the library door closed behind her, Toria pushed sleep and comfort from her mind. She pulled Sarnai's notebook closer and leaned over the text, spinning the pen Kane had removed through her fingers. She reviewed Zhinu's notes, establishing that she'd had no luck deciphering Sarnai's code using additional metrics.

Sarnai wrote in Loquella. Of that, Toria had no doubt. The extra symbols present anywhere in the text must represent common mathematical shorthand.

This entire time, their attempts at code-breaking had emphasized the text itself. Zhinu's facility with languages, including her fluency in multiple forms of writing that employed varying written styles, had come in handy in combination with Toria's ability to sift through information. But Zhinu admitted with no embarrassment that math had never been her strong suit, so they had ignored the equations until now.

But once upon a time, Toria studied chemistry at Jarimis University as part of her concentration on metallurgy. Chemical equations used math as a core language, so Toria ignored the other writing for now. She snagged a fresh sheet of notepaper and flipped through the book, copying each equation to isolate them from the surrounding text.

What she found made no sense.

To be fair, the work Sarnai performed at the lab soared far beyond the work Toria did in college, and the last time Toria had done a deep-dive into anything science-related, it had been geological in focus. But math was math.

A quick perusal of the library turned up a physics primer, and Toria spent an hour giving herself a crash-course in basic equation structure for that discipline. However, when she returned to Sarnai's notes, they continued to confound her. Might as well have been written in Qin.

Except the Qin language in its written form crossed the page from top to bottom, then right to left. Whereas Loquella read left to right, gifting Toria with a near-permanent streak of ink across the side of her hand throughout her entire education thanks to her left-handedness.

Though Toria's dominant hand belonged to a genetic minority, Sarnai's birth tongue made much more sense to her from a writing standpoint since it wrote from right to left.

She dove for Sarnai's notebook.

It could not be that easy.

A rush of adrenaline banished the exhaustion from Toria's mind, and with a careful hand, she reversed each of the equations. A bit at a time, logic slotted into place.

She returned to the first page of Sarnai's notebook using the first in the list of basic code structures she and Zhinu compiled. This time, she treated the original text as if written in the Chingis style.

She found success with the fifth code, even as the letters on the page swam—this time, from lack of sleep.

Toria dropped her pen with numb fingers and bolted from the library. She shouted for Zhinu and forced excitement through her link with Kane. She sprinted up the stairs to Rob and Zhinu's suite and pounded at the door. "Wake up! I broke the code!"

Footsteps echoed from both directions, and Rob flung open his door at the same time Kane sprinted toward her across the gallery.

Zhinu darted under Rob's arm, trailing a half-donned dressing gown in her wake. "Show me!"

Leaving the men to chase after them, Toria chased Zhinu to the library and pointed between the cipher pattern and the paragraph of decoded text. The information itself did not instill excitement, consisting of a short to-do list. But with the puzzle solved, the rest of the notebook's contents were in reach.

Toria divided the clean copy of the notebook's contents into quarters, thrusting them at each of her companions. They clustered around the central library table, using whatever writing utensil and plain paper came to hand. Once she explained how to use the correct cipher in conjunction with Sarnai's backward writing, they dove into the work.

Though adrenaline had warred with Toria's exhaustion and come out the winner, she welcomed the mug of coffee Mrs. Hamilton placed at her elbow. She murmured an absent thanks, not sparing further attention from her work.

"Woke for my day and realized you lot were still hard at work," Mrs. Hamilton said. "Did you ever get to bed?"

"Toria never did," Rob said, flipping between two pages. "I hope you gave her straight espresso."

"You know how I feel about that nonsense." Mrs. Hamilton drew the curtain open at one of the library's windows, and rays of dawn poured into the room.

"Everyone stop for a moment." Zhinu followed her own order by exchanging pen for mug. "Anything interesting so far? I've got the first bit, and it's mostly lists of the grunt work they made the poor girl do as the office newcomer."

"Until she starts working exclusively on a transportation project," Kane said. He showed them a sheet covered in equations. "The math might as well be Qin to me—no offense, Zhinu—but she did a lot of research into the satellite system under development. Working out payload mass and flight trajectories."

"For the communications systems, right?" Zhinu asked.

"I think so," Kane said, stretching in his seat until his vertebrae popped.

"No, that's not right." Rob compared one of his pages with Kane's work. "It's not a communications satellite. Which is weird because that's what I'm paying for. Sarnai's work here indicates that the payload includes some sort of temperamental substance, and her new task is protecting it from inertial forces and temperature variations. Some sort of explosives? Perhaps for a secondary propulsion system."

"But that implies a longer-range mission." Kane accepted the paper from Rob and scanned its contents. "Pushing a satellite farther away in orbit defeats the point of expanding radio communications that depend on line-of-sight."

As Rob and Kane debated the requirements outlined in the lab's original proposal for such a project, the roar of puzzle pieces fitting together in Toria's brain drowned them out. Her work on the last section of the notebook revealed a Sarnai who understood she needed to keep her work hidden. A woman under strict orders not to discuss the project with other lab members, despite her safety concerns.

"Because the project no longer has anything to do with communications," Toria said, cutting off a question from Zhinu. "The rocket isn't carrying satellite equipment anymore. They weaponized the explosive propulsion elements. And Sarnai's last project was when Tierney forced her to work out the trajectory for targeting Roman territory. The town where Tierney's brother died."

Rob reacted to Toria's revelation with understandable shock and outrage, pacing the library and spluttering invectives, leaving Toria to explain the necessary context for Kane and Zhinu.

"We have to stop this, obviously," Zhinu said. "We can't let Tierney get away with murdering people."

"She's already murdered someone," Toria said. "I imagine she's responsible for Sarnai's death if Sarnai threatened to expose her plan."

"I need to get to the lab," Rob said.

Mrs. Hamilton clapped him on the shoulder before he could escape the library. "No, you lot need to get some proper sleep. When is this thing scheduled to launch?"

"Three days from this evening." Rob pressed his palms to his face. "You're right, as always, Mrs. Hamilton. I'll be a menace on the road if I leave now."

Toria volunteered right away to finish the translation, which the others met with a resounding denial. Once Kane threatened to toss her over his shoulder to force her from the library, she relinquished her pen with reluctance. Her partner chivvied her into a hot shower, and despite the coffee, she had no problem passing out next to him afterward.

After the much-needed sleep, they gathered in the parlor that let in the most afternoon sunlight. They had decisions to make.

"As much as I want that woman hauled away in chains," Rob said, picking at a sandwich, "I have a responsibility to my board. They'll need to know what's going on before this incident hits the news cycle. I'll have to alert my public relations crew, get the legal team involved—"

"And amend our contract if you want us to do the actual dirty work," Kane said, ever the practical one. "And don't forget that the more people know what's going on, the greater the risk that Tierney will get alerted and either go into hiding or do something drastic."

"More drastic than dropping a pile of explosives on an innocent town?" Zhinu asked. Before Kane replied, she lifted a hand. "No, you're right. I can already think of even more ridiculous options the woman might have tucked away in that lab."

Rob counted off tasks on his fingers. "I can get a lawyer here tonight with a new standard Guild contract for the two of you. Get my assistant to arrange an emergency board session for tomorrow morning, and call my communications director to organize a press conference for the afternoon."

"And by then, you'll either be reporting that Kane and I have turned Tierney over to police custody," Toria said, "or something much worse that I don't even want to contemplate." She itched to race for the lab and confront the scientist. To put to rest the spirit of the young woman Toria might have befriended in another life, a woman who might have risen through the ranks to direct cutting-edge projects with Zhinu and Rob's patronage.

"Well, she's got no chance against the three of us," Zhinu said.

Toria coughed, a bite of sandwich caught in her throat at Zhinu's pronouncement. "Not at all."

The other woman bristled. "You can't presume to think I'd let you go into danger and leave me safe at home?"

"You're still under house arrest, love," Rob said. "The last thing we need is for you to be the center of attention when the real danger is out there."

"Everything could backfire if the confrontation with Tierney fails," Toria said. Zhinu's glare of betrayal struck her to the core, but Kane's practicality had rubbed off on her over the years. "Think of how it would look if Tierney gets away. What if she puts out the word that you were after her the same way you killed Sarnai?"

"But everyone knows I didn't kill the girl!"

"The public doesn't," Rob said. "And the optics are what matters here."

"Besides, we're still under contract to be your bodyguards." Kane shoved his plate away, food half-eaten. "Rule number one of bodyguarding is not to drag your body into unnecessary danger."

Zhinu's restlessness fled. She placed both hands flat on the parlor table and dug sharp blue nails into the varnish.

But paint did not color the weredragon's nails. And when Toria switched her attention to Zhinu's eyes, her vibrant blue irises shimmered in the afternoon sun.

"Last I checked," Zhinu said, her voice echoing with the preternatural tones created by her heritage, "I was a blessed dragon. Born to a royal house. And a hell of a lot less destructible than the two mages hired to protect me." A sapphire tinge rolled across her face and arms, a ripple of scales that settled into human skin.

Rob's own eyes echoed gold, and a trace of growl undercut his response. "I will not allow my wife to endanger herself."

Toria and Kane may as well no longer be in the room. If she didn't know better, she would fear an explosion of fur and scales at any moment. Instead, the couple stared each other down, two dominant, volatile beings. Toria resisted the urge to push her chair back from the table. To make any movement at all and attract either fierce gaze.

Rob folded first, but not by backing down. Instead, he leaned over the table corner that separated him from his wife and grasped her face in both hands. "You will be safe. You will not take any unnecessary chances. You will not risk your freedom."

"I won't risk my freedom," Zhinu said. "I won't let anything keep us apart."

They kissed, and Toria sent a wordless query to Kane.

He returned a silent confirmation.

Zhinu's words to Rob said nothing about risk, and if anything, her vow to him promised even more mayhem.

But having a dragon on their side as they returned to Foundry Laboratories, where they would face robots and who knew what other scientific horrors, did not disappoint Toria in the least.

Weredragons had ruled the Qin empire for thousands of years. Generations of pride and power created beings with the ability to command the might of a throne room, a stadium of spectators, or an army of thousands. The lone security guard at Foundry Lab's gatehouse all but trembled before Zhinu's imperious might. He waved them through without argument. The uniformed woman in the front lobby fared no better.

When Dr. Meredith Tierney arrived in her office, promptly at the six-thirty start to her day, Zhinu sat behind her desk. Zhinu had chosen a tailored business suit for the confrontation, the image of modern professionalism.

Zhinu's distinct appearance marked her as foreign, and her presence at the lab was known. With no way to hide her as another mercenary, she demanded to play herself in this scheme. In contrast, Toria and Kane braced each side of the desk, decked in combat gear, weapons, and their versions of the grizzled mercenary scowl.

Toria itched to draw her sword and shove the blade to Tierney's throat, demanding a confession. To bring closure to Sarnai's death and peace to the girl's soul. But she promised to follow Zhinu's lead.

And to be fair, Zhinu herself brought a lot of power to the table. With any luck, they would manage to force Tierney into custody with no blood spilled.

Tierney paused inside her office, squinting through the late spring dawn that spilled through the window and cast her welcoming committee in shadow. She studied the waiting tableau as she placed her large purse atop a bookshelf loaded with thick binders. "Good morning, your ladyship," she said. "Forgive my tardiness. I was unaware we had a meeting this morning."

Zhinu tapped her chin with one finger. "My presence here was not scheduled. But my husband and I became aware that one of your current projects does not fit the specifications presented to the government oversight committee. We decided it was in everyone's best interest to allow you to correct the error before it becomes public knowledge."

The scientist did not flinch. Toria shifted her weight but kept her arms loose at her sides. She doubted that a person who already had blood on her hands would admit guilt with so little persuasion, but she had seen stranger things. Perhaps Tierney would accept this exit strategy. The police would still have to collect evidence pinning her to Sarnai's death, beyond the journal's contents. But from what they had deciphered, the changes Tierney ordered to the payload and launch trajectory of the rocket would be more than enough proof of attempted mass-murder.

"I see," Tierney said. "How unfortunate that my planned launch alterations were not communicated to the committee effectively. I'd be happy to discuss any updates with you so you can assure your husband of my dedication to the project."

Kane stepped forward, an echo of his adrenaline surge pulsing through Toria's veins. But Zhinu thrust an arm ahead of him as she rose from the desk chair. "I'd be more than happy to discuss your revisions to the launch plan."

With the briefest of glances at the two mercenaries, Tierney led Zhinu through the deserted halls. They traced a familiar path outside the administrative building and crossed to another building on the facility grounds instead of to the more massive structure that housed the rocketry components.

As if Zhinu shared the same mental link that projected Toria's concern to Kane, she asked, "Are you not escorting me to the assembly building?"

"That's not where launches occur," Tierney said, as she used her access pass to unlock the exterior door. "We have already transferred the rocket carrying the communications satellite to the launch pad deeper on lab property. This building is where we will conduct all ground operations."

She escorted them down a brief hallway and into a room that contained spectator seating for perhaps a dozen officials, facing a reinforced window that showed a larger space lined with rows of computers. Toria stayed at Zhinu's shoulder and scanned the area with magesight but found no sign of anything living. Instead, the faint static of electrical current buzzed along her skin, evidence of the massive number of electronic components housed in this building.

Under Zhinu's fierce stare, Tierney stepped to a small computer tucked in one corner. She woke it from sleep mode and typed commands into a screen that crawled with code.

"This is the command center for the launch?" Kane asked. He finished his circuit of the room, even checking inside the cupboard that supported an empty water cooler.

Tierney did not move from her work. "In the other room, yes. I'm afraid you don't have the necessary clearance to go further than this."

Zhinu huffed in irritation. "I'm sure we can both agree that my status in the Wallace family provides all the clearance I could need."

Her shoulders tightened, and Tierney said, "I'm transferring the necessary data to this machine for your review."

Toria tried to track what Tierney typed as green text scrolled across the black screen. Unfortunately, what little she understood about operating a computer did not extend to whichever programming language the lab used for the satellite program. For all she knew, Tierney could be ordering them coffee from the lab's cafeteria.

Zhinu wandered to the window and placed her hand upon it. Her fingers flexed, and her blue nails clicked against the glass.

After another few seconds of typing, Tierney backed away from the computer. "If you'll excuse me, your ladyship, I need to get the rest of the data from another machine. You and your escort are welcome to remain here until I return."

"Kane, go with her," Zhinu said.

"That won't be necessary." Tierney pointed in the other room. "I'll be right there, within sight."

Though Kane had already left Zhinu's side to accompany the doctor, Zhinu said, "Alright." Kane froze mid-step, and his combined irritation and confusion lashed Toria's mind.

But Zhinu's agreement made sense. Right now, all Tierney knew was that they suspected—something. But not what, or to what extent. So, they would play nice and learn what tidbits of information Tierney might part with until they could make a move.

Tierney acknowledged Zhinu with half a bow and exited, tugging the door closed behind her.

Toria lunged forward, but not quick enough. The heavy slam echoed against the cinderblock walls. When she whirled to face the other room with Kane and Zhinu, the doctor appeared as promised.

Zhinu smacked the flat of her hand against the window. "What is the meaning of this, Dr. Tierney?"

The doctor paused in the midst of waking various computers in the room. She spoke, her voice muffled but intelligible through tiny grates set above the window. "Your presence here has forced me to accelerate my timetable. Unfortunate, but necessary."

Fury sharpened Zhinu's voice. "Did you kill her to cover up your plans to fire upon an innocent Roman town?"

Tierney did not suppress her flinch. "Ms. Khan's death was an unavoidable sacrifice. Like your own will be."

"Shit," Toria said. She tried the door latch. It refused to turn under her hand.

Zhinu pounded the glass, but Tierney no longer acknowledged her. She typed on another computer and exited the room. When she did not reappear, Zhinu rolled her shoulders and turned to Toria and Kane. "Can't say I'm surprised, but it would have been nice to be proven wrong."

"Tor, can you zap the door?" Kane asked. "No reason to stick around and wait for whatever she decides to throw at us."

"My thought exactly," she said. She hovered both hands over the metal door latch and caught Kane's lance of power. With a mental twist, she funneled the energy through herself. The force targeted the lock mechanism.

The electronic portion of the lock fractured and fried beneath her onslaught, but when Toria tried the latch again, it remained stiff. "No luck," she said. "She engaged a physical bolt when she left. Window?"

"The glass is at least an inch thick, and it's threaded with steel mesh," Zhinu said.

"Shouldn't be too hard between both of us," Kane said. When Toria joined him at the window, the dim lights in the launch control room brightened, and the remaining computer consoles powered on. The electronic hum against Toria's skin, which she had mostly ignored, strengthened to an uncomfortable itch.

The computer in the corner beeped once, and Toria spun to face it. A large number onscreen replaced the scrolling code: 900. When she checked the computers in the other room, the number repeated on each glowing screen, in vibrant green font against black.

"Nine hundred what?" Zhinu asked.

With repetitive, steady beeps, the number changed. Eight hundred and ninety-nine. Eight hundred and ninety-eight.

"Seconds," Kane said. "It's counting down. Fifteen minutes."

Toria pecked at the keyboard. She hit the "enter" button, then typed "stop" and "cancel" and "close." The number continued to descend. "Fifteen minutes until what?"

Kane unfocused with a distant expression. He pushed his sleeves to his elbows and crouched where he stood, placing both palms flat against the scuffed linoleum floor. The new tattoo on his forearm glinted with magical traces, but Toria ignored how it churned her stomach.

"The ground is shaking," her partner said. "Just enough."

Toria's stomach discomfort turned to lead. "Oh, hell," she said. "It's a damned countdown."

"Not to what I think it is?" Zhinu asked.

"Something is about to launch," Kane said, straightening and tugging at his sleeves. "The question is, what?"

The locked door shuddered as a weight crashed into its opposite side. Toria concentrated electric power in her right hand as she drew her rapier with her left, and Kane unsheathed his scimitar half a beat behind her.

The deadbolt slid, and the door swung open. When Zhinu made to step forward, Kane forced her aside.

But it wasn't Dr. Tierney who returned, nor any other humanoid shape. Toria bit down a yip of fear as five of the robotic figures tumbled into the room, mock feet searching for grip on the linoleum floor in their haste. The last robot used its upper limb to slam the door closed behind them.

The four-legged construct in the lead extended its prehensile limb, and blades sprouted from the blocky mock fist. Despite the lack of eyes, whatever senses these machines possessed scanned the room. The static hum against Toria's skin pulsed.

"These are what attacked you before?" Kane asked.

"Yeah," Toria said. Though the wounds had healed, their memory scraped her raw. "One of them. And one of them was probably all it took to kill Sarnai."

"We don't have time for this," Zhinu said. She shrugged off her suit jacket and kicked her low heels into the corner of the room.

Older weredragons possessed the ability to transform shape with their clothing, but Zhinu did not yet have that skill. But it appeared that her time with her husband and other werewolves had rid her of any Qin modesty she might still possess, even if her transformations had remained private.

The countdown beep softened in comparison to the roar of electricity that pulsed along Toria's magical awareness. The five machines remained steady, even as Zhinu stripped. Toria hesitated to engage the constructs with Zhinu unprepared, but she said, "These things might have cameras. You're about to reveal your secret if they're broadcasting to an external source." The British government knew, which meant it was already a matter of time before the Qin figured out they had lost a treasure—a female weredragon capable of shifting form. Any additional risk compounded the odds of that inevitable conflict happening sooner rather than later.

Zhinu unhooked her bra and dropped it atop her discarded clothing. "My secret is not worth the lives of innocents." Cerulean scales rippled across her exposed skin as she spoke, accompanied by the gruesome sounds of bones breaking and reforming. But Zhinu's face expressed no pain as her human form shifted, and soon a sinuous weredragon fell to four clawed feet where a bipedal once stood. Her tail lashed, shoving two of the chairs against the far wall.

The robotic dogs never twitched. When Zhinu spoke again, through an extended jaw that should not have been able to shape human speech, she directed her words to the robots that had waited through her transformation with uncanny patience. "You waiting for us to strike first?"

"Probably, if their command was to keep us in this room." Toria forced aside the urge to keep herself between the robots and her charge, but the razor edges of their claws would find less purchase against Zhinu's scales than they had through human skin.

The electronic buzz faded, replaced by warm earthen energies as Kane funneled power from the ground and fed it to Toria. The energy that gathered in her off-hand strengthened, forming a knot of ball lightning. She chanced a momentary glance at the innocuous computer in the corner. The number had fallen below seven hundred. This standoff did nothing but waste time.

Exactly what Tierney wanted. "If we're getting out of here, it's through them," Toria said. She raised her hand and discharged the lightning into the lead construct. Electricity lanced through the room, and Zhinu snarled, a hair-raising predatorial growl.

That much power should have reduced the mechanical beast to charred wreckage. Instead, the electricity rippled across metallic skin. One of the four legs froze with a scratchy whir. But the other three and the fifth upper limb rumbled to life, and it stepped toward Toria, dragging the dead leg. "They're shielded," she said, scrambling backward.

"Rubberized skin," Kane said. "We'll have to do this the old-fashioned way." He swung at the construct nearest to him with a snarl of his own, tangling his sword with the blades that extended for him.

Toria dodged the cluster of blades that swung at her and transitioned the movement into a low attack, stabbing the vicious point of her rapier into an exposed joint where leg met body on these strange machines. "Zhinu, watch your left!"

The blue dragon lunged to the side, catching another robotic dog with her claws and crushing its bladed fist. The knives crumpled in her grip like tin foil. That took care of one attack method, but it caught Zhinu's forelimb with its frontal limbs. Metal pounded her scales, and Zhinu hissed through her fangs at the brute force of the blows.

"We have to get out of here, Tor!" Kane swept his blade at another robot, throwing his weight behind the blow. Sparks flared, and the robot jerked to the side. It crashed against the window glass, where spiderweb cracks formed.

Toria dropped to one knee as the fifth limb swiped in her direction, and she used both hands to force her sword point into another exposed joint. This time, she threaded power through the blade itself. The energy met no resistance, and the machine froze mid-movement as Toria's magic fried the electronics with prejudice. She wrenched her sword away as the construct collapsed, unable to compensate for its unbalanced state.

The harsh tang of burnt plastic mixed with ozone swept through the room. Toria sneezed.

Her brief moment of inattention almost proved fatal. One of the robotic dog forms waiting in reserve crept forward at its brethren's demise. This one did not have a fifth limb extending from its torso and instead used one of its legs to sweep at Toria's crouched form. Zhinu launched herself at the creature. They skidded across the floor in a tangle of limbs, biological and mechanical, until they collided with the table holding the computer.

The screen toppled and shattered, but the beeping continued unceasingly.

Zhinu collected herself at the same moment Toria stood. The remaining robot appeared to consider both women and decide it would have more luck aiding its final cohort against Kane. The other warrior-mage engaged his first opponent in a game of cat and mouse, teasing the blade cluster with openings before dodging for a blow of his own. The blocky body sported a multitude of scores from Kane's scimitar, but none of them appeared to have diminished its capability.

"Help Kane." Toria climbed over the fallen robot. She had to get that door open. They had no idea how far away the rocket sat on the laboratory grounds, and none of them had the computer skills necessary to cancel the launch from this command center even if they broke free.

Zhinu blocked her with her larger form. "Don't be an idiot." Her inhuman face expressed recognizable irritation as she continued, "Brute force will do where your magic failed."

Toria had to stop thinking of Zhinu as the petite woman she had been hired to protect. In her dragon form, Zhinu was stronger by orders of magnitude. She didn't waste time agreeing with Zhinu, charging toward Kane while the slam of a large body against metal reverberated through the room.

Toria and Kane needed no communication to fight side-by-side. This time, she thrust power at her partner, and he used the energy to bolster his shields. When the robot lashed out with its arm, it hit an invisible barrier that crackled with electricity instead of the edge of Kane's scimitar.

Talons shrieked against metal as Zhinu continued her battle with the door. The two remaining robots had no chance of defeating the combined strength of the warrior-mage pair. Kane and Toria just had to figure out how to disable them first.

Kane's intention flickered through Toria's mind a split second before he made his move. Toria's turn to attract the constructs' collective attention. She dropped her arm to her side, lowering her rapier out and away, and faced the robots—exposed and defenseless.

Whatever controlled the fake beasts contained no sentient intelligence. Such a blatant trap would fool not even the lowliest mercenary apprentice. But the two robots pulled their attention from Kane in favor of the obvious target.

As mechanical constructs, not sentient foes who might sense the thrum of power building in the air even without magical senses of their own, the robots had no way to understand that Toria wove strength into her shields. Kane's earthen energies, pulled from the ground below the building, reinforced the crystalline structures that vibrated with pure storm power.

When the first robotic leg stepped into the space Toria had claimed for her domain, shock reverberated through the metal body. Not enough to short out the electronics, but it scrambled for balance rather than pressing the attack. The second blundered into its companion, tripping over the scrabbling legs and distracting whatever passed for its brain into a fight for balance of its own.

Toria stepped forward, forcing her shields along with her. Like shoving a boulder up a hill, the constant rumble of power continued to distract the robots as they attempted to coordinate their limbs.

Kane slipped around the jostling robots. His magic had never been as flashy as Toria's, but the subtlety of earth packed as hard a punch as the fiercest storm. This time, when he slammed his scimitar into the robot's unguarded rear, he channeled the power Toria forced through her shields into his blow. Where before his sword had left gashes on the metal shielding, this hit cracked the metal like a nut. His blade drove into the mechanical innards, tearing through a swathe of circuitry and gears.

Hydraulic fluid sprayed from the construct, spilling like false blood. Kane's attack on its cohort attracted the second robot, which turned away from Toria to the new threat.

The tattoo on Kane's arm sparked with power, and he released his sword with one hand to throw out a palm. Toria shoved the shield toward him.

Neither of them touched hand or sword to the final robotic beast. But the power of their shields made physical crushed it between their concentration. Its limbs twisted and broke, and by the time Toria released the excess energy on her end for Kane to ground, the creation moved no more.

A gust of fresh air dispelled the odor of singed electronics and oily hydraulic fluid. The metal door hung in shreds as if ripped open by a giant can opener. Zhinu crouched nearby, worrying at one talon with her teeth.

"Good job," Kane said to Toria, even as he sheathed his weapon and accepted the scaly limb Zhinu offered him. He pressed one hand against her wounded talon, and the air pressure in the room shifted as Toria's hypersensitivity to Kane's magic caught his use of power. When he finished the short healing, he released Zhinu. "Time check?"

Toria peered through the fractured glass into the launch control room. "Five hundred thirty-seven. And counting."

Zhinu snaked her long neck through the carved opening. "No one in sight. We have to find Tierney. And stop the launch."

"We can't waste time. We need to split up." Kane crouched to touch the ground again. "The vibration is still there. I'll go for the rocket. You two find Tierney."

Having Zhinu at her rear was better than nothing at all, but the idea of separating from Kane and leaving him to face any other robotic beasts did not sit well with Toria. And then there was the obvious. "How the hell are you going to stop a missile from launching?"

"Hopefully, I'll figure it out by the time I get there." Kane shifted through the rough opening, careful not to catch on any of the sharp edges. Zhinu and Toria crawled out behind him.

The door they had used to enter the launch control building itself remained unlocked. Kane knocked his forehead to Toria's temple and tossed a wave to Zhinu before he loped across the manicured lawn in whatever direction he sensed the earth's disruption. Her gut clenched when he vanished behind another building on the sprawling campus.

The earth screamed in pain, where it burned. Kane's lungs burned, too, as he sprinted across the field toward the launch tower. Ignition would not occur until seconds before the actual launch, but the earth remembered. More than one launch had already scorched the land around the tower.

Kane played a dangerous game. He had to get close enough to the rocket to stop it. If he failed to prevent the launch, the explosion might outright kill him. Or he might suffer blast trauma that his healing ability would be powerless to fix.

This would be so much easier with Toria by his side. Even now, her concern-fear-support leeched into him, buoying his confidence before it could flounder in a sea of terror.

152

But the last thing they needed was for Zhinu to end up in the blast zone. Rob would murder them himself. Better for her and Toria to chase the doctor. What was more strange robotic creatures compared to the might of a rocket laden with explosives?

Kane jumped from an embankment, a human-made dam of dirt and rock manicured to appear natural. In reality, it acted as a buffer zone between the laboratory's main campus and where the launches occurred. A road might exist to transport the rockets, but he weighed the risk of putting a foot wrong in a burrow against the wasted time seeking a more stable route.

There. A metal tower, three stories tall, supported the upright rocket. Its metal skin gleamed in the light of the rising sun. Under normal circumstances, a flurry of workers would perform checks and double-checks and triple-checks, ensuring that this advancement in British communications technology survived its trip intact and launched technological progress forward.

Instead, Tierney intended the rocket to be a vehicle for destruction.

And Kane had to stop it.

He slid to a halt on the dewy grass a few hundred yards from the tower. How much time had his run cost? Unbidden, a number flashed through his mind via Toria. One hundred and sixty-four.

He had fewer than three minutes to prevent this rocket from launching.

Kane extended his arms at the launch tower and activated magesight. Though the understanding of alloys and mechanics fell under Toria's talents, metal was another form of earth, and he read that well enough. The new tattoo on his arm glowed gold even beneath his sleeve, and he threaded power through it.

In the Londinium park, it allowed him to ground power with little effort. Out here, surrounded by a landscape almost untouched by man, the tattoo sharpened his magesight. His ability to sense the earth threaded through the launch tower's metal until the entire structure glowed with inner power.

Now he had to figure out what to do with that power.

The tattoo extended his ability to sense the earth but not manipulate it. The last time he faced a technological horror, he severed its power by cutting away the biological connection between the missile and the tattooed mage. He had no such shortcut available this time.

What would Toria do?

Together, he would feed her power, and she could summon a storm with the might of a hurricane from the clear sky. It would muck up the local weather pattern for weeks, but the churning clouds would provide enough power for Toria to strike it with lightning, forcing billions of watts of energy through the metal tower and rocket until they were a smoldering wreck much like the robots she had fried.

But he did not have Toria. And this was not a battle he could fight with sword alone. Right now, Kane was nothing more than an earth mage. Earth mages tended toward the power of healing. The power of creation.

But the earth also had the power to destroy.

Kane fell to his knees and sank his fingers into the grass. Where the earth had screamed in pain at its memory of previous launches, he stoked that pain. Converted it from fear to anger.

Before he sensed movement beneath himself, a flock of birds launched itself from a distant grove of trees. They screeched as they wheeled through the sky, and moments later, a wave of various rodents—mice and hares and voles—scrambled through the field and away from the launch tower.

Now, the vibration reached a strength evident to human senses. As Kane stared at the launch tower, the land it stood on burned with a different sort of power.

For the briefest moment, Kane longed for Archer by his side instead of Toria. The water mage's unique talents would serve them well here. Together, they could liquefy the earth itself and swallow the entire launch structure whole.

But Kane stood alone against the horror of the explosion to come, unless he could destroy it first. He channeled power through his own body, streaming it into the ground to command it to his will.

Below, the earth woke.

"Oh!"

Toria paused at Zhinu's outburst but did not lift her hands from either side of the doorknob. Zhinu's senses had tracked Tierney to this building, so this was where they needed to go. "What? What's wrong?" Toria finessed the electronic system that secured this entry to the central scientific building with deft mental fingers.

"You can't tell what Kane is doing?"

"Not exactly." Zhinu wanted to talk about this now? Toria had work to do. The energy buildup that rumbled beneath her skin, evidence of whatever power Kane controlled elsewhere, was a minor distraction at best.

"We're about to be in for a wild ride."

The door popped open with a burst of static shock, and Toria flexed stiff hands. With her curiosity prodded by Zhinu's words, she snuck through the warrior-mage bond to try to figure out Kane's plan. A rocket paired with a tall launch structure appeared in her mind. It rippled, but not from artifacts in Kane's vision. The earth itself trembled in anticipation.

Not in anticipation. Kane primed the earth with his power. Soon, the ground would move in an area not known for strong natural earthquakes.

Arguments against that had to exist, in much the same way Toria was careful with manipulating local weather patterns. But today, need outweighed caution. "He knows what he's doing," she said. "We have our own job."

She led Zhinu into the building; both women stayed on alert for more robotic foes Tierney might arrange to block their path. Was it her imagination, or did the tremble in her body echo the force of Kane's will?

Kane's handling of earth energy trended to plant growth and healing. Toria used the flashier magic in combat, and he supported her with a line of power and brute strength with a sword.

He had never caused an earthquake before. Never done anything like this before.

The tower swayed. Metal ground against metal in shrieks of abuse. The shudder of movement swept across the structure. Soon, the roar of the earth itself overpowered the screech of battered metal. If Kane had not caused the maelstrom, he would have covered his ears. Instead, he powered through, cycling earthen force back into itself, feeding the frenzy he found leagues below as it rippled through the planet's crust.

How much time did he have left? Raising such power had required as long as he expected, but much longer than he wanted to spare. But when he poked at Toria again, a frantic response of unknown-busy-anger rang through their link. She faced her own problems at the moment.

Now, when the earth moved, Kane could no longer attribute it to his imagination. His position on his knees allowed him to maintain a semblance of balance instead of getting tossed to the grass.

The structure swayed further, a broken pendulum.

How much more would this take? How strong an earthquake would Kane need to produce to disrupt the rocket?

And how much damage and injury would he cause in the surrounding area to save the lives of faceless Romans hundreds of miles away?

For all Tierney's intelligence, the woman lacked an element of common sense. From the shock that painted her face when Toria and Zhinu burst into the laboratory, she had assumed a cadre of mindless beasts and a simple wooden door had the strength to contain two warrior-mages and a fucking dragon.

Color Toria unimpressed.

Tierney froze, her hands poised above another computer keyboard. Toria yanked her away from the work station by the elbow. She sensed another time check request from Kane, but her priority lay in shoving Tierney against the nearest wall and pinning her forearm across the woman's neck.

The building rattled as if in echo of Toria's anger. "How do I stop the rocket launch?"

"There is no stopping it." Tierney did not struggle in Toria's grip. "I've bypassed the standard control system. My code controls the launch sequence, and I didn't program an abort method."

The room quaked again. A coffee mug danced off the edge of a nearby desk. When it hit the cement floor, it shattered into ceramic shards.

"I didn't imagine it," Zhinu called from the other side of the room, where she busied herself ripping apart anything that resembled another robotic creature. "Kane is summoning an earthquake."

"Good. He'll keep the rocket from launching."

But Tierney laughed, a full bout of hilarity that left the woman shivering. "He's as good as dead. The fuel primed to ignite once I sent the signal."

"What the hell are you talking about?" But Toria's knowledge of explosives already gave her the answer.

"Even if it doesn't go anywhere, that missile is exploding."

From Sarnai's notes, Tierney had designed the missile to devastate a small town. "Then you're as good as dead, too," Toria said. "Unless you tell me how to stop it."

Tierney sagged against Toria's hands. "If I can't get justice for my brother, I might as well be dead already."

Melodramatic much? Toria allowed the woman to collapse to the floor, where her shoulders continued to shudder with laughter. Or was it the jostling from the earthquake that vibrated the lab?

One thing was for sure—many more people were as good as dead if that missile exploded on the ground. Toria needed to communicate with Kane. Not enough time to track him down on the laboratory grounds, to find the launch site. Which meant connecting with Kane's mind from beyond physical contact. Something she had never accomplished before.

"Zhinu, watch our friend here." Toria sank into a cross-legged position on a clear stretch of floor.

The weredragon picked through the robotic detritus to loom over where Tierney slumped. A lone woman had no hope of escaping a dragon standing guard. "What's happening?"

"I need to talk with my partner."

If Zhinu responded, Toria did not hear. She tuned out as many external stimuli as possible. She kept her position loose, riding the quaking earth like a fractious horse. She drew inward, tunneling within herself to seek out the kernel of Kane's soul that resided within her own body, her own mind.

The farther apart they were, the more their connection grew tenuous until the information Toria received boiled down to the immediate fact that her partner lived. From a few miles, they could transmit the barest emotional imprints. Their current distance made basic information possible, such as the previous time request. At a few feet, even more detailed impressions passed through their link, and when touching skin to skin, they had managed outright telepathy on a handful of occasions. Under controlled circumstances, with few distractions.

What Toria attempted now should not be in her grasp. But their lives depended on it.

Kane's life depended on it.

She slipped through his shields, mental and magical, like passing among the shadows under a thick forest canopy. Careful not to distract her partner from his mission, she approached at a metaphorical angle. Kane sensed her proximity and linked their mental hands. Adrenaline-fueled determination from both sides slammed them together until her own body was a distant sensation.

Her eyes opened. But her view did not include a sinuous blue dragon crouched near a huddled woman.

Sunlight poured across a lush field, where emerald power rippled across the landscape.

Her forearm itched.

But not her forearm.

Toria?

Kane. We have a problem.

His partner's voice echoed inside his skull. Kane's right arm tingled, and he tugged up the sleeve of his cotton undershirt. The new tattoo glowed with power, twisting greens and purples so bright that they might even be visible without the magesight that colored his world with energy.

"How can I hear you?" His voice disappeared under the earth's continuous growl. But speaking the words aloud helped sharpen the power behind his query, and he hoped the mental connection ran both ways.

Not the right question. Fear-irritation-anger colored Toria's thought, none directed at him, along with a touch of amusement, which was.

But before he could ask the right question, information blossomed in his brain. Toria's conversation with Tierney compressed into a memory packet, which unfolded into a perfect picture of their current mess.

So even—? Kane shot a return package along the link without bothering to frame words, comprised of his plan to vibrate the earth hard enough to rattle the rocket from its launch tower and disrupt the trajectory even if it managed to launch.

Right.

Another mental flash: the world consumed by flame, encompassing him and overwhelming his shields, leaving him a burnt husk among the charred field. Toria's imagination ran wild, spinning out into a possible future where she sprinted across the molten ground before collapsing like an abandoned marionette.

He reeled her back in, centering her attention on the problem at hand. They would fix this before it got that far. Kane had no plan to die today.

So, toppling the rocket would not be the quick fix he assumed. The close connection Toria bridged between them opened another source of power, and he poured more energy into destabilizing the earth.

Shock-confusion-amazement, this time. No words, because this was outside the realm of Toria's experience—like her manipulation of weather patterns was all Qin to him.

Trust me. No need to make it a question.

And in return, the most straightforward response: *Yes.*

The roiling power coalescing at Kane's forearm burst. The spots in his brain and magic and soul he identified as Toria swelled as she surged into place. And for the first time in his life, Kane was whole.

The ground bucked.

Their hands flickered where their fingers splayed in the grass. Petite and pale one moment, wider and dark the next. And when they looked up, two versions of magesight battled until the strengths of both won out. Earthen currents showed where the ground's weak points existed to be exploited, and electrical power shimmered through the missile and launch tower, pulsing along prescribed pathways.

And where they could alter those pathways.

We need more power.

Britannia was not a land of earthquakes. It had been quiescent, settled into its current state, for thousands of years. An occasional restless moment shivered the dirt, but otherwise, the earth was content with its form and resistant to change.

Part of them wanted to apologize to the earth for waking it from its peaceful slumber and asking of it such an enormous feat. But they did not ask the lightning for its fierceness; instead, they guided it through new paths and reveled in its strength. Thus, they would beseech the earth for this favor and remind it of its ability.

Remind it that it was the literal bedrock upon which the rest of the world stood. That the thing they sought to destroy was a creature of its birth, forged from elements mined from this source. And that what the earth gave, it had every right to rescind.

The ground itself boiled beneath them, and the tide turned. The physical realm melted away in their mingled gaze. The alien structure clung to its surface like a poisonous leech. If it wanted to fly away and spread death elsewhere, why should it be stopped?

No! they cried, and thrust visions of destruction into its slumbering mind.

Britannia might be an island, but it remained part of a whole. The earth had already suffered millennia of the mites on its back. They chewed into its skin and dumped poison into its blood.

They were its children, and if they wanted to save it, it had to trust them.

All of a sudden, the power they poured into the ground through their hands, fingers digging into the dirt, became like a trickle compared to the wave of force that slammed upward. They clung to the grass as the land bucked beneath them.

The rocket and its launch structure, a slurry of miasma that blotted out the intensity of the elemental energies saturating the world, shattered and crumbled. The earth rose to meet it, gaping jaws opening to absorb the blight into itself.

They could do nothing at this point but hang on for the ride. The launch structure sank into the earth. Electrical power, running through ground conduit, surged for a final time.

A secondary shockwave shook beneath their feet, shooting clots of dirt and charred rock from a geyser-like spout where the launch structure once stood. They curled into a ball, protecting their head with their arms and shunting their remaining energy into an arc of shielding.

Finally, the earth stilled.

They peeked between their arms. Fractured arcs of raw earth ran through the surrounding grass. In the distance, the lab buildings remained whole, though not without visible damage. Cracks in the siding and missing shingles showed the landscape had not survived unscathed.

But the most significant evidence that the earth had gone to war on their behalf was the rocket itself, and its launch tower. Both were just—gone. All evidence of technology had vanished, leaving a churned mess of dirt and asphalt behind.

They uncurled, ignoring the complaints of aching muscles, and lurched to their feet. A wave of dizziness washed over them until Toria adjusted to the unfamiliar height.

Their forearm itched again, and when they checked it, the new tattoo had shifted. A wash of cloud formed a new background to the tree structure, and bolts of lightning entwined the branches, curled around the trunk, and splayed amidst the roots.

It was perfect. It was them.

But it couldn't last.

Toria slammed into her own body. Her back ached, and she winced against the brightness of the morning sun. "How the hell did I get out here?"

"I dragged you. Thought the building might collapse on us."

She angled her head until Zhinu came into view. The stretch popped vertebrae in her neck, and she groaned at the release of tension. She rolled onto her side and struggled to her knees.

Zhinu, still in dragon form, crouched over Tierney's body.

"She still alive?" Toria asked.

"Yes." The sibilant of the word edged into a snarl. "A shelf almost fell on her. I shouldn't have pulled her out with you."

Unspoken, the idea that a dead Tierney solved many of their problems. But it introduced new ones, too.

And her forearm still itched. With a growl of her own, Toria shoved up her sleeve, ready to attack the irritated skin with blunt nails.

A new pattern spread along the inside of her arm. Not the ghosts of veins beneath her skin, but ink within the skin itself. The clouds and lightning that had appeared among Kane's new tattoo. Now, the image settled onto her own body as if she'd carried the ink for years.

Well, fuck. Toria didn't hate it. The design appealed to her and might have been the sort of art she would choose for herself if she decided to get a tattoo that announced her magical alignment to the world.

Except she hadn't.

She needed to talk with her partner. When they did not have to contend with the fate of a murderer. "We have to alert the police. Let them know what happened here," Toria said.

"Did you not notice the epic earthquake?" Zhinu asked. "I imagine the local constabulary have enough to deal with at the moment."

"Exactly." Toria staggered to a standing position, pulling her sleeve over her arm's new decoration. Out of sight, out of mind. For now, at least. "And we're at the epicenter."

The lab had not been deserted, despite the morning's early hour. They needed to check on the security guards and find out whether anyone else worked early today. As if someone had read her mind, the peal of a fire alarm echoed throughout the grounds. That should get everyone mobile out of the damaged buildings. Now, they had to worry about anyone trapped under furniture or other debris.

At their feet, Tierney stirred.

They did have to figure out what to do with Tierney, with or without the cops. Toria considered and dismissed ideas as fast as they formed. Their best bet was contacting the police standing watch at the Wallace estate, still none the wiser that Zhinu had escaped the premises stashed in the trunk of the vehicle Kane and Toria left in. After all, no reason for them to keep Zhinu under watch now that they have the real killer.

And there was that gleam in Zhinu's sapphire eyes. Not the familiar spark of curiosity. Not even the bright glint that heralded amusement.

For the first time, Toria stood in the shadow of a predator.

But she was not the target.

The unconscious woman twitched again, but Toria and Zhinu locked their gaze above her body. Despite the boundaries of culture, upbringing, and even species, they arrived at a wordless accord.

Zhinu flexed her claws again. She lunged for the scientist.

No!

Acting despite her intention to allow Zhinu this choice, Toria lashed out and caught the slick scales of Zhinu's forearm. Their previous link had broken, but her partner's voice echoed through her mind once again.

Don't do it!

"Kane?"

He limped around a nearby building, streaked with dust. "Don't do it!" he repeated aloud.

Zhinu twisted out of Toria's grip. With a whip of her tail that gouged a divot in the grass, she spun to face Kane. "Why shouldn't I? She killed first. I will avenge an innocent woman's death and protect this realm from the further machinations of a madwoman."

But Kane focused his attention on Toria as he approached. Even as she shared the weight of his exhaustion, his compassion overwhelmed their link. It balanced the outrage and contempt Tierney inspired in Toria. "We don't kill people," he said. "Not anymore."

Sirens wailed. Police vehicles lurched to a halt at the main Foundry Labs building as Toria rounded the corner. Kane followed close, carrying Tierney over his shoulder in a fireman's hold. He dumped her to the ground on the main drive, and the woman stirred.

Three officers arrowed in their direction with weapons drawn. Toria raised empty hands, palms out, and Kane mirrored her.

"Don't shoot!" Toria's voice echoed across the open area, loud in the post-earthquake silence that continued to ring in her ears. "This woman is Dr. Meredith Tierney. She's responsible for the death of Sarnai Khan."

Tierney twitched at their feet as she stirred. Even though Kane had stopped Toria and Zhinu from killing her, the chance existed that Zhinu's blow had caused permanent damage. The rational part of Toria's mind hoped the woman would repeat her confession and clear Zhinu's name.

Another part would not grieve if Tierney never again managed a coherent sentence.

The plainclothes officer stepped forward after holstering his weapon, leaving his compatriots to guard the figure at their feet. Toria recognized him as the person in charge of the attachment protecting the Wallace estate. "Lady Wallace is no longer at her residence, Master Connor. I don't suppose you have any idea as to her whereabouts?"

They had left Zhinu around the corner, back in human form and wrapped in a lab coat for modesty's sake. Kane figured it wise to keep her out of sight until evidence confirmed Tierney's confession.

Except another man climbed out of a police cruiser.

"Shit." Kane pitched his curse low. Toria echoed his sentiment.

"Kane. Toria." Earl Wallace rushed toward their awkward cluster, every inch the nobleman despite his casual clothing. "I'm glad to see you well. I feared the worst during the earthquake. Please answer the detective's question. *Where is my wife?*"

Toria considered and disregarded half a dozen possible responses while Kane vibrated with tension next to her. But none of her potential answers became necessary when a white-clad figure darted past and threw herself into Rob's waiting arms.

Rob spun Zhinu around with the force of her embrace and kissed her the moment he sat her down. "I found your note," Rob said when they broke for air. "I was so worried."

"We're fine, all of us," Zhinu said. "And we caught Tierney. But she wasn't just a murderer. It was worse. So much worse."

As if on cue, Tierney groaned. Two police officers kept their weapons trained on her as she woke, and she flinched away from the morning sun.

"Can you hear me, Dr. Tierney?" the detective asked. "Do you require medical attention?"

Tierney propped herself up on her elbows. "That dragon bitch assaulted me," she said, her voice like gravel. "She ruined it. You all ruined everything."

"She requires medical attention," Toria said, cutting off Tierney's tirade before she built more steam. "And her lawyer."

The police helped Tierney off the ground and cuffed her before leading her to one of the police cruisers. Kane turned to Rob and Zhinu once they passed out of earshot. "Rob, you're going to need your lawyers, too. And your PR team. Call everybody."

Rob's arm around Zhinu's shoulders tightened. "I don't suppose this was a natural earthquake, was it?"

"No," Toria said. "And it's no longer about a murder."

Toria escaped to retrieve Zhinu's clothing from the launch building, and the trio gave full statements to the police. It was all over but for the shouting.

The sun crept over the tree line. Lines of sweat tickled Toria's skin, under her armor. She wanted to get out of the bright sun, but they had no way to determine the structural stability of the surrounding buildings. The earthquake had been localized to the surrounding ten or so square miles, but that included an entire nearby town. Rob demanded that emergency services focus there instead of on the vacant laboratory buildings.

Toria and Kane rested on a patch of grass outside the Foundry Labs main building, with front row seats to the explosive row between their nominal charge and her husband.

"I never want to wake up like this again."

"We left you a note."

"A note is a poor substitute for sacrificing family honor on the altar of your one-woman crusade."

"I wasn't one woman. I had backup."

"You snuck out of the estate under of the noses of your security detail."

"My prison-keepers, you mean."

Kane pressed against Toria, so they sat shoulder-to-shoulder. "Have to get it out of their systems, I guess."

Toria gestured to the police, who at this point had stopped pretending not to eavesdrop and instead stared at the raging couple with open interest. "They could do without the audience, though."

"You going to interrupt that?"

"Nope."

Magic continued to hum between them, aftershocks of their connection. According to a pair of officers who had ranged out, nothing remained of the rocket or launch structure but a field of churned earth the size of a rugby pitch. Eventually, they would have to detangle the threads, but Toria wanted nothing more than to lean into Kane's calming presence after such an intense morning. Except such a close rapport meant keeping some thoughts locked away.

Zhinu was half a second away from interrupting Rob's lecture about public trust in the noble class. Despite her human form, Toria imagined the ghost-like image of a draconic tail whipping side to side. But when Kane spoke, his words gripped Toria's attention in a vice.

"No more death. This is the last job then, huh?"

No need to explain. Kane had been in her mind. "When the Romans invaded, they brought human resources and trucks and crossbows and swords. The antique nuclear warhead was a fluke." Toria waved one hand in the general direction of the former launch complex. "But now power like this exists in the world. The Romans will find out a rogue element in Britannia meant to attack them. Even if they don't retaliate, they'll increase their defenses. Word will spread. To the Qin. To the smaller powers in the south."

"We can't let Limani get left behind."

"No, we can't."

Toria straightened, and her spine cracked in protest. Without the physical touch, she slowed the process of withdrawing her magic from Kane, ignoring the streaks of cold that slid through her limbs as Kane did the same. "And I miss Liam."

There it was, finally, out in the open. The acknowledgment that after her trip to the past, she could no longer live the rest of her life leaving loved ones behind.

"Yeah," Kane said. "I miss Archer, too."

Officials in Londinium lifted all charges, actual and pending, against Zhinu. Sarnai Khan's father made no effort to speak out against her in public, so against the wishes of pretty much everyone, Zhinu insisted on visiting the man to offer condolences for his loss.

"He kicked her out, you know," Toria said, as she rode with Zhinu in the rear of the town-car toward the apartment block that held the Khan family home. "She wouldn't follow the plan he set out for her, so he threw her away like she was nothing."

Zhinu stared out the window at the shabby neighborhood. "The Chingis hold different views on religion than my own, but our people come from the same root society. We retain some similar cultural practices. I hold partial ownership in the company that employed the woman who murdered Sarnai. It is my responsibility to offer compensation for the man's loss."

They spent the rest of the ride in silence. The visit itself was brief. Kahn and his wife greeted Zhinu in a front room cluttered with family pictures and religious iconography. Zhinu spoke a few words in Qin and bowed before the parents. Sarnai's mother thanked Zhinu for her time in halting Loquella. Kahn said nothing at all. They left.

Gan awaited them outside, leaning against the building's bare brick. A jolt of tension thrummed under Toria's skin as Kane stopped, blocking Zhinu.

"How did you know we were here?" he asked.

"Fancy car like that on this street? Only one person it could be." Gan bowed low to Zhinu. "Your ladyship," he said, followed by a string of Qin.

Zhinu laughed and gestured for him to rise. "Not the correct phrasing for a woman of my rank, but I appreciate your effort." She switched to Qin, and Toria recognized a few of the same phrases from upstairs. Zhinu grasped Gan's hand before he could sidle away and continued in a more insistent tone. As the one-sided conversation progressed, Gan's face paled.

They blocked the flow of traffic on the sidewalk, but the pedestrians allowed them a wide berth, all staring at Zhinu as they passed. Finally, she released Gan's hand. "Please say you'll think about it."

Gan glanced up for a brief moment, as if he could peer through walls into the Kahn family apartment. "I will think about it, your ladyship."

"That is all I ask." Zhinu turned to the town-car, and Toria hastened to open her door.

When Gan waved Kane away, he returned to the driver's seat. Kane pulled the vehicle away from the curb, then flicked his gaze to them in the rearview mirror. "Mind if I ask what that was all about?"

"I intend to establish a nonprofit that focuses on allowing the Chingis community to reach their full potential as part of British society while retaining their cultural heritage," Zhinu said. "I invited Gan to be my first employee."

Silence reigned. Kane's mind touched Toria's and prodded her to respond. As if she coped better than her partner with emotional issues. "That sounds like a great plan," she said.

"I'm sure you noticed that I didn't make a proper scion of British nobility during the short time before my arrest," Zhinu said. "I had my fill of acting the decorative political object back home. Now that I'm out of school, it's time to do something productive with my time."

Toria found no fault in any plan that kept her from holding up ballroom walls and supervising backstabbing gossip disguised as a garden party. "When do we start?"

As Zhinu directed, Kane drove to the offices of the Wallace corporate lawyers. In less than an hour, Zhinu had changed the parameters of their bodyguard contract, and he would be lying if he didn't echo the relief-intrigue-excitement from Toria's end of the link. But old habits die hard, and he entered the building's ultra-modern lobby first. A security officer noted their arrival from his station. A trio of suits stared at Zhinu when she breezed in in behind Kane. Toria followed at the rear.

Zhinu pointed out the coffee shop tucked in one corner of the lobby. "No reason for the two of you to sit through boring meetings. Why don't you relax there?"

Kane bit his tongue instead of asking whether Zhinu was sure. "Want us to get you anything?"

"I'm sure the offices upstairs will have any beverage I might desire," Zhinu said. "But thank you."

"Shout if you need us," Toria called as Zhinu swept to an open elevator, her heels clicking on the smooth tile.

Zhinu flicked her fingers in acknowledgment, then vanished from sight as the doors slid closed.

The partners stood in the lobby. Neither moved.

"This is weird," Toria said. "Is this weird?"

He commiserated with her mental urge to follow their charge wherever she might lead, but Zhinu brooked no interruptions to her newfound independence. "It's weird." Now, the suits stared at him and his partner instead. "Let's go sit."

Toria ordered drinks while he selected seats from the scattering of café tables. Kane's chair had an unobstructed view of the front doors. Toria would see the entire elevator bank. He continued to suppress the itch that prompted him upstairs and into position outside the law offices.

After all, Zhinu was a weredragon who had proven herself more than capable of protecting herself. They had never been more than window-dressing, and in a way, acknowledging that fact lifted a load from his shoulders.

Toria set an iced coffee in front of him and dropped into her seat. "So, what next?"

Such a multilayered question. "Today, or in general?"

"Both, I suppose." She sipped her drink. "Today is Zhinu's problem. After this contract, though…what would you think of going home to stay?"

She kept her posture loose, but Toria leaked a thread of nervousness-excitement-curiosity beneath her casual demeanor. He had known this conversation loomed in their future. Had even settled on an answer over multiple sleepless nights, staring at the ceiling above his bed. "I've never felt the same aversion to kids as you. I'd be more than happy as a full-time teacher at the school with Archer. But I know that's not for you."

Toria swirled her drink, watching the ice clack in the glass. "I'd keep pitching in where needed and mentoring the air mages. Maybe another storm kid will manifest soon. But honestly, I don't think the school needs three full-time instructors."

True. Last year's crop of new apprentices included one more student than the previous year. The numbers grew but continued to be low. "I know you have other passions."

"Right." Toria perked up. "Despite all Tierney's shenanigans at Foundry Labs, so much there is cutting-edge research. I meant what I said about not wanting Limani left behind."

"The university."

"Exactly," Toria said. "It's already a leader in academics. The perfect pipeline for a research institute."

A snippet of Toria cuddling robotic puppies flashed through Kane's brain, a vision not created by his own imagination. "You're ridiculous."

"I try. The world spell is gone. Who knows where the limit is now?" Toria spread her arms, encompassing the coffee shop, the building, Londinium, farther still. "Limani's always been special. We can compete."

"We have to."

Toria raised her half-empty drink. "To the last job?"

Kane clicked his glass against hers. "To home."

EPILOGUE

Their six-month contract with Zhinu had ended the day before. They board a ship for the New Continent the next. But today, Toria had one final mission before leaving Londinium.

The lightning swarm tattoo that coalesced on her skin during her close connection with Kane faded in the days after the earthquake. Toria then spent the next five months distracted by the blank expanse on her arm, a low level of constant surprise at its nakedness.

If she was going through with it, this was her last chance.

She knelt on a pallet as Tuya organized her pots of ink. Kane lurked in a corner, and he snatched his hand away from his earthen tattoo when he caught Toria staring.

"You sure you want to do this?" he asked for the third time since leaving the Wallace townhouse. The seventh time since Toria confessed her urge the night before, asking him to call Gan and arrange the appointment with Tuya.

Tuya responded in Toria's stead. "She's sure, child." She pointed at the door. "You're hovering. Go. Make sure Gan served tea for her ladyship before work distracted them."

Zhinu and Gan waited at Tuya's kitchen table, poring through responses to a renovation proposal for the building that served as the center for Chingis cultural events. Public opinion of the Chingis people remained cool since Zhinu became the face of community relations endeavors. However, the locals in the center's immediate Londinium neighborhood verged almost on lukewarm these days.

When Kane hesitated, Toria nudged him through their link.

As he thudded down the stairs, the thrum of Kane's nerves dimmed with distance. "Thanks," Toria said. "I think I'm ready."

Tuya laid a selection of brushes on a towel. "Lie back, and let me in."

Toria stretched flat on the pallet, shutting her eyes but opening a sliver of her shields to Tuya's gentle power.

Tuya settled warm hands on Toria's forearm. "Breathe with me, child."

She followed suit until her breathing echoed the same pattern as Tuya's, and she dropped into a light meditative state. At the first whisper of a brush against her skin, her presence spiraled further downward.

But she did not panic at the sensation. No reason to.

Their eyes opened in Tuya's warm kitchen, where they sat at the table opposite Gan and Zhinu. They cupped large hands around a mug of warm tea. Relaxing, though lending half an ear as their friends sifted through paperwork and discussed ideas.

Love spread through their core, connecting the central point that linked them. It might require a touch of strange magic to complete the full circuit, but this affinity would never be unnatural.

Hey, it's you.

It's me.

Limani and their partners called to them. But now, on some level, they would always be home.

Acknowledgements

This book benefited from the valuable comments and insight provided by Chelsea Stickle and Jennifer Della Zanna. Thanks for always taking this wild ride with me.

The ride got wilder in 2020, and I'm privileged to work with Jennifer Barnes and John Edward Lawson, who supported me when I asked to throw the original plan out the window and then suggested options for making the new plan even better.

Julia Vilece and David Brawley provided invaluable encouragement (and memes). Lee Murray provided endless optimism (and kind words). Lauren and Chad Ferguson provided support (and wine). Danielle Brannock and Dylan Landress provided friendship (and escape). And even though he once again claims to have nothing to do with my crazy writing life, Erik continues to provide me with the love and space necessary to enjoy it to the fullest.

Photo by Brian Roache

ABOUT THE AUTHOR

By day, J. L. Gribble is a professional medical editor. By night, she does freelance fiction editing in all genres, along with reading, playing video games, and occasionally even writing.

Previously, Gribble studied English at St. Mary's College of Maryland. She received her Master's degree in Writing Popular Fiction from Seton Hill University in Greensburg, Pennsylvania, where her debut novel *Steel Victory* was her thesis for the program.

She lives in Ellicott City, Maryland, with her husband and three vocal Siamese cats. Find her online (www.jlgribble.com), on Facebook (www.facebook.com/jlgribblewriter), and on Twitter and Instagram (@hannaedits). She is currently working on more tales set in the world of Limani.